Pearl

(Part 1)

by

Arianne Richmonde

About this novel.

Pearl, follows Arianne Richmonde's bestselling books in *The Pearl Trilogy: Shades of Pearl, Shadows of Pearl and Shimmers of Pearl*; the tumultuous and heart-rending love story between forty-year-old documentary producer, Pearl Robinson, and French Internet billionaire, Alexandre Chevalier, fifteen years her junior.

The book that Pearl Series fans have been asking for: the flip side of the tale. The story according to Alexandre Chevalier.

At only twenty-five, Alexandre Chevalier is a billionaire. His social media site, HookedUp, is more popular than Twitter, more global than Facebook. With his devastatingly handsome looks, alluring charm, and his immense wealth, he has women falling at his feet, desperate for his attention. But his heart is set on only one woman: Pearl Robinson.

Alexandre's dark and dysfunctional past makes him crave stability and a normal relationship, but he soon finds out that Pearl is a bird with a broken wing. Why, he isn't sure.

Pearl is written from Alexandre's point of view from the moment he and Pearl first meet on a rainy summer's day in a coffee shop in New York City.

In any relationship details are hidden; things are left unsaid. Not all conversations are remembered in the same way.

And not all actions are disclosed—especially to the one you love most.

Part 2 of ***Pearl*** to be released October 2013.

Praise for *The Pearl Trilogy:*

'A heart wrenching love story you won't forget.'
—*E McDonough*

'There is one regret I have about reading this series—that I waited so long to read it.'
—*Nelle L'Amour,* bestselling author of *Undying Love*

'If you like *50 shades of Grey* and the *Bared to You* series, you are ABSOLUTELY going to LOVE *The Pearl Trilogy*. The books are addictive, heart pounding, suspenseful, sexy, and steamy!!! So if you are jonesing for an erotic read that will keep you on edge, hot and bothered, with an amazing love story. I highly recommend *The Pearl Trilogy.*'
—*Books, Babes and Cheap Cabernet*

'I loved the older woman/younger man dynamic of this book! It's about time this kind of story was written. A strong older woman and an equally strong young man fall in love and overcome insurmountable odds to be together. *The Pearl Trilogy* has that and more. The twists and turns in the story only add to the intensity. The attraction between Pearl and Alexandre is palpable and borders on obsession. The love scenes are passionate and raw. *The Pearl Trilogy* is the complete love story from beginning to sweet end and I enjoyed every single word…'
—*Martini Times*

'The best erotica series I have read to date.'
—*Megan Cain Loera*

'What an amazing series this was. I recommend you give this one a nice long read. *The Pearl Trilogy* will knock your socks off. Getting to know Pearl and Alexandre is definitely a must. Arianne Richmonde is a very talented story teller.'

—Mary Elizabeth's Crazy Book Obsession

'*The Pearl Trilogy* is a must read!! OMG! I loved the Fifty Shades and Bared to You series…but this one is a topper!! I laughed and cried – it's so well written. So many twists and turns and just when you think you know where this story is going….you don't! Now, if only I could meet a hot Frenchman like Alexandre Chevalier…'

—A.J Cox.

'All three books flowed wonderfully and had the perfect ending for the wonderful trilogy. If you haven't read this yet, put it on your Must Read list!! I look forward to more from Arianne Richmonde!!'

—Sassy and Sultry Books

'I was completely entrenched in this story. The descriptions. The emotions. Between the mystery, the lies, and the hot sex… my head was literally spinning and going to explode.'

—Love N. Books

'A FREAKING awesome story filled with so much drama…oh, how I loved the drama. It was a big page turner for me and when things got crazy oh how I got sucked in!'

—Momma's Books Blog

'We loved the plot and also the secondary characters in *The Pearl Trilogy*. The author does a wonderful job of developing their stories, too, and we LOVED the journey these books took us on. The storyline is great and the sex scenes do NOT disappoint. Mrs. Richmonde also gives us lush scenery and exotic locales, and there are a LOT of plot twists. Trust us, you will NOT anticipate the twists and turns of this story.'

—*The Book Bellas*

'I am a fan of the 50 Shades of Grey series and the Bared to You series. I thought this was better than both of them put together. I found a new author who can't write fast enough. Arianne Richmonde is a new fave for me.'

—*Reviewer*

'The main attraction here is that Pearl is so true to life. She goes through the same life struggles we all talk about with our own girlfriends. What a change from the twenty year-old virgins in other erotic novels. As for Alexandre, I found him so sexy. Are there any men out there really like him I kept asking myself?' You'll love the series, too, if you believe a woman doesn't have to be in her early twenties to find love and passion.'

—*Shades of Momma*

'The twists and turns that happen in this book are amazing – some stuff you just don't see coming. You have to read this book if you are looking for something that isn't your typical book!'

—*WhoAreYouCallinABookWhore*

'Awesome; full of heart, tears and much laughter. This book flows together and feels so real and true I forgot I was actually reading a story. I love these characters. If you want to read something great, get these books.'

—*Dawn M. Earley*

'This book has twists and turns that I never expected. I thought this might be another knock off of Fifty but Oh, no! This book holds it's own and I loved every word of it!'

—*Samantha Addison*

'Wow, this had me on the edge of my seat, or rather, bed. I have loved the whole trilogy of Pearl. I love how this author writes, she made me believe I was watching the whole thing like a film in my head which is just how I like to read my books, watching them play out and imagining the characters.'

—*Confessions of a Bookaholic*

'I couldn't turn the pages fast enough. I was cheering for team Pearl/Alexandre. This book was HOT and sexy. Ms. Richmonde gave the reader a little of everything. The secondary characters made the drama and suspense of this book.'

—*Wine Relaxation And My Kindle*

'This is how a true erotic story should be; great story line, wonderful characters, and some of the **HOTTEST** sex/love scenes I've read. This is where the author's writing shines. I could really feel the attraction and desire that Pearl and Alexandre had for each other. Their chemistry was amazing and their need for each other leapt off the pages. Arianne Richmonde did a wonderful job, not with just the story and characters but also with her skillfully crafted descriptive writing. The whole Pearl Trilogy has simply captivated me.'

—*Swept Away by Romance*

'At times the trilogy had me laughing so much. I absolutely LOVED how the author's dialogue pegged how the characters spoke. The Pearl Trilogy is so worth the read...don't miss out!'

—*Sugar and Spice Book Reviews*

'The twists and turns left me in pieces or angry enough to want to throw my kindle. Other times, it was so sweet or incredibly sexy that I didn't think I'd be able to get enough. I found it very hard to put it down. *The Pearl Trilogy* is a definite page-turner and absolutely loved the way it ended. I am very much looking forward what Arianne Richmonde releases in the future.'

—*The Book Blog*

'I was hooked on this book from the very first page. I had many mouth hanging on the floor moments because I was just so surprised as to what I was reading. I swear you won't see it coming.'

—*The Book Enthusiast*

Formatted by: BB eBooks

About the Author

Arianne Richmonde is an American writer and artist who was raised in both the US and Europe. She lives in France with her husband and coterie of animals.

As well as ***The Pearl Trilogy* series** and ***Pearl*** she has written an erotic short story, ***Glass***. She is currently working on her next novel, a suspense story.

If you have not already read ***The Pearl Trilogy*** which proceeds this book, all books are available in paperback:

The Pearl Trilogy bundle

Shades of Pearl

Shadows of Pearl

Shimmers of Pearl

To be advised of upcoming releases, sign up:
http://ariannerichmonde.com/email-signup

For more information on the author visit her website:
www.ariannerichmonde.com

Dedication

To every one of my amazing readers who asked for more of Pearl and Alexandre. Thanks for all your love, support and feedback. ***Pearl*** would not have been possible without you.

1

It was raining in New York City. The sort of rain that felt vaguely tropical because it was summertime and the muggy heat was broken by a glorious downfall. Very welcome, because my sister and I had just given a talk at an I.T. conference and she was feeling hot and bothered—really getting on my case.

The rain eased the tension.

Sophie was driving me nuts that day. It wasn't easy going into business with a sibling, but if it hadn't been for her shrewd business savvy, I wouldn't have had the same luck. Sophie inhaled HookedUp. Exhaled HookedUp. Being as obsessed with money as she was, she wouldn't rest until we'd practically taken over the world. And, as everyone now knows, social media really *has* taken over the world so she was onto something big. Clever woman.

Sophie had moved our conference talk forward by an hour because she was in a foul mood—wanted to get it over and done with—get the hell out of there. I, on the other hand, felt bound by some odd sense of duty to share our success story; inspire people to jump into the deep end as we had done. To go for it.

At the conference, someone in the audience asked me how I would describe myself and I replied: "I'm just a nerd who found programming fascinating. With a keen eye for patterns and codes, I pushed it to the limit and got rich. I'm a lucky geek, that's all." People laughed as if what I said was a silly joke. But I meant it.

I'm still not used to being a billionaire. Even now, if I ever see an article written about the power of social media and HookedUp, it's as if I'm taking a glimpse into someone else's life; a driven, ambitious, 'ruthless businessman' (as I've often been described), when I'm still just a guy who likes surfing, rock climbing and hanging out with his family and dogs. Just an ordinary man. Others don't perceive me that way—at all. I suppose I should be flattered by their attention, although I'm a private man and hate the limelight.

I took a chance, worked hard, and got lucky. A Frenchman living the American Dream.

That's what I love about American culture. Everybody gets a shot if you get off your ass and have the will to succeed. Not so in France. It's hard to break away from the mold; people don't like to see others rise above their station. Maybe I'm being hard on my country, judgmental, but all I know is if I'd stayed there, HookedUp wouldn't be the mega-power it is today. Not even close. The USA has given us all we have and I'm grateful, even though having this much money still feels sinful at my age. Or any age, for that matter.

Funny how Fate pans out; you never know what life has in

store for you.

I nearly didn't go into the coffee shop that day. Sophie needed a shot of caffeine and I really wasn't in the mood to argue, so we dashed in from the rain and stood in line.

Our conversation had been heated, to say the least. We'd been discussing the HookedUp meeting we had scheduled in Mumbai in a couple of weeks time. It was a mega-deal that she'd been feverishly working on all year. I didn't think HookedUp could get any more global and powerful than it already was, but I was wrong. That deal was going to make us silly money. Really silly money. I knew I was going to be able to buy that Austin Healey I had my eye on. Hell, I could have bought a fleet of them. Aircrafts too. Whatever I wanted.

Sophie took out her Smartphone from her Chanel purse and said in French—her voice low so that nobody would overhear, "Look, Alexandre, this is the guy we're meeting in Mumbai." She scrolled down to a photo of a portly man with a handlebar mustache. "This is the son of a bitch who's squeezing us for every dime. He's our enemy. He's the one we need to watch."

"But I thought you said he's the one we're signing with—"

"He is," she interrupted. "Keep your enemies close." She brushed her dark hair away from her face and narrowed her eyes with suspicion—a habit I had myself. I remember thinking how elegant and beautiful she looked; yet in 'predator mood,' she was also formidable. I was glad to have her on my side.

Half listening to my sister gabble on about the Mumbai deal, I noticed a woman rush through the door—a whirlwind of an entrance. She was flustered, her blonde hair damp from the summer rain, her white T-shirt also damp, clinging to her body, revealing a glimpse of perfectly shaped breasts through a thin bra. I shouldn't have noticed these sorts of things, but being your average guy, I did. She was battling with an enormous handbag—what was it with women and those giant handbags? What did they carry in those things—bricks?

"Arrête!" Sophie snapped and proceeded for the next couple of minutes to berate me for not paying attention. She was rolling her eyes and puffing out air disapprovingly. Ignoring her, I wondered, again, why I had gone into business with her because she was really bugging me. She added, "If you want to fuck that girl you're staring at, you can you know—American women put out on the first date."

I hated it when my sister talked like that to me—it made me cringe—especially her sweeping generalizations about other countries and civilizations.

"She doesn't strike me as that type," I mumbled back in French. The pretty lady was now closer and I couldn't take my eyes off her. She had her head cocked sideways and was staring at the coffee menu, chewing her lower lip in concentration. She was beautiful, like a modern version of Grace Kelly—she looked about thirty or so.

My eyes raked down her perfectly formed body. She was dressed in a tight, gray skirt which accentuated her peachy butt. The slit on the pleat revealed a pair of elegant calves, but her chic outfit was marred by sneakers. Somehow, it made her all the more attractive as if she didn't give a damn. As my gaze trailed back up to her breasts, I saw that she was wearing an *InterWorld* button. *Good,* I thought, *we have something in common—I can chat her up.*

I cleared my throat and moved a step closer. "So how did you enjoy the conference?"

She jumped back in surprise; her eyes fixed on my chest. I felt as if I was towering above her, although she was a good five foot six. I looked a mess—T-shirt and old jeans with holes in the knee. So far, she was not responding. I knew that New Yorkers could be just as rude as Parisians so I wasn't fazed.

She flicked her gaze at me but said nothing. I was right—she hadn't answered my question, just continued to look at me; stunned, as if she really didn't want to have a conversation at all.

I smiled at her. I felt like a jerk, but dug myself in deeper. "Your name tag," I said. "Were you at that conference around the corner?" I decided that she obviously thought I was a total jackass as her response was clipped, terse.

"Yes I was," is all she said and then cast a glance at Sophie.

I realized that this woman—her nametag said **Pearl Robinson**—must have assumed that Sophie was my girlfriend—the perils of hanging out with my beautiful sister. Or maybe Pearl Robinson wasn't smiling simply because she wanted me to shut the hell up and leave her alone.

But I didn't back off. "I'll pay for whatever the lady's having, too," I told the girl serving our coffee. I wanted to say, 'Whatever Pearl's having' but thought that Pearl would peg me for some kind of stalker. Why I continued to pursue her I wasn't sure, since she was clearly not interested. But I couldn't help myself. "For Pearl," I added, wondering why I was not getting the response I was after. Not to be arrogant, but women did normally smile at me, if not give me the eye. They still do. Daily. But Pearl was not buying it. I wanted her to flirt, brighten up my dull day.

I went on, undeterred—for some reason I didn't feel like giving up; she had really piqued my interest. "Pearl. What a beautiful name." *Jesus what did I sound like? A typical French gigolo type, no doubt.* "I've never heard that before. As a name, I mean."

In my peripheral vision, I caught Sophie rolling her eyes, again, and she whispered in French, "Bet you anything you'll have that woman on her back in no time." *Shut up!*

Pearl Robinson finally reciprocated with a beautiful big smile. *Nice.* Pretty teeth. Sexy, curvy lips. She told me about her parents being hippies or something—explaining her name. I wasn't listening. I'd got her attention, that's all I cared about. I could tell she liked me. *Took long enough for her to warm up, though—all of forty seconds.* I felt triumphant. Why? I met pretty women all the time. But there was something about this one that really captured my attention. She was poised and elegant, yet unsure of herself. There was a childish, vulnerable quality about her which I found disarming, even beguiling. She was rifling through her enormous handbag, trying to find her wallet. Why are American women so keen on paying for themselves? Was she embarrassed because I was buying her a coffee?

"What's your name?" she asked, while simultaneously staring at my nametag.

Good…ironic sense of humor, I thought. I laughed and introduced myself. Introduced Sophie, too.

Pearl went to shake Sophie's hand and her wristwatch caught on my T-shirt. I looked down at her other hand. No wedding ring. *Good.* I felt my heart quicken with the physical contact of her delicate wrist brushing against my chest—the intimacy—and I knew….in that nanosecond, I knew; I was going to have to fuck this girl.

The way she was looking at me was giving me the green light. Yet her big blue eyes were unsure of me. She looked down at the floor, and then up again at me. She may not have even known it herself at that point—women rarely do—but she wanted me to claim her. I could almost hear her screaming my name. I pictured myself pinning her up against a wall, all of me inside her.

I wanted her. And I was going to have her. You bet. Every last inch of her.

"Remember to use protection," Sophie whispered in French, "she may look like an nice Upper East side WASP, but you never know."

I retorted, also in French. "Get your coffee, or whatever you're drinking, and *leave* because I've had enough of your snippy conversation for one day."

Sophie cocked her eyebrow at me and smirked. I turned my attention back to Pearl Robinson and prayed that her French was limited or non-existent. I gazed at her, right into her clear blue eyes. *Yes,* I decided, *I want this woman.*

And she wanted me. I was pretty damn sure. She was jittery, nervous, tongue-tied—couldn't get her sentences out straight. Why? Because I was running my eyes up and down her body, mentally undressing her, and she could sense the electricity. The heat. She was all flustered. She could read my mind. She was fumbling for something in her monster-bag again. Her apartment keys, she told me. Was she planning on inviting me over?

"Nice to meet you, Pearl," Sophie said, giving her the once-over. "Maybe see you around some time?" The innuendo was so thick you could have cut it with a machete.

Sophie sashayed out of the coffee shop and I exhaled with relief. *Thank God, now I can get down to business. Real business.*

"I got the drinks to go, but do you want to sit down?" I suggested to Pearl. She nodded.

Why I was so taken with this New Yorker, apart from her obvious good looks, I wasn't quite sure—she had a quirky kind of charm. I liked her. And I decided right there and then—I didn't just want to fuck Pearl, I wanted to get to know her, too.

She eased her way into an armchair but was unsure whether to cross or uncross her legs. Like a schoolboy, I found my eyes wandering to her crotch and imagining what lay beneath, but she was too demure for that. Her legs crossed closed, and she smoothed that sexy pencil skirt over her thighs. I thought about fucking her again—I couldn't stop myself. I wondered if what Sophie said was true: that Pearl would put out on a first date. I'd have to find out….

We were interrupted by a phone call from my assistant, Jim, telling me to snap up the Austin Healy I'd had my eye on—they'd accepted my offer. So the conversation with Pearl swung around to cars. I felt like a jerk. I knew what women were like; feigning interest about bits of machinery when they really couldn't give a damn. Pearl was no different. Still, she did a good job of pretending. She nodded and smiled and widened her pretty eyes. Meanwhile, I had one thing on my mind: to get her into the sack ASAP.

But then she took me off guard. She started talking about reruns of old sitcoms, classic novels, and old songs and I began to think we had something in common besides physical attraction.

Then, when I mentioned my black Labrador, Rex, that was it. I began to mentally tuck my tackle back into my pants, so to speak, because she admitted that she was crazy for dogs, too. She loved the fact that I could take Rex to restaurants in Paris and a flash of our future ran before my eyes. I swear. I had a vision of us together eating something delicious, Rex at our side, and something told me that Pearl and I would make the grade. It does sound crazy, that. Call it a premonition—I think it was.

She was telling me about her childhood Husky.

"My dog was called Zelda," she said, her liquid eyes flashing with happy memories.

"Like Zelda Fitzgerald?" I asked. "Scott Fitzgerald's wife?"

She looked up at me, surprised. "Yeah, you know about her?"

"Of course I do. She was a little bit crazy, wasn't she? *The Great Gatsby* was partly inspired by her."

"Well, like Zelda Fitzgerald, our Zelda was a little out to lunch. I mean, literally. She loved chickens. Went on several murderous escapades."

"The way you say that with a little smile on your face makes me believe you didn't have much sympathy for the innocent, victimized chickens," I teased.

"They were going to be slaughtered anyway, poor things." She put her hand on her mouth as if she'd put her foot in it. "Sorry, Alexandre, are you a vegetarian?"

I loved the way she said *Alexandre* with her cute American accent, trying to accentuate the *re*. "No, you?"

"No red meat. Only organic chicken. I know…kind of ironic considering what Zelda did. I do have a conscience—I'm against intensive farming, you know, animals spending their lives in tiny cages, so small they can't even turn around. Cows being forced to eat grain, not grass—being pumped full of antibiotics. People don't like inviting me to dinner. I'm a tricky customer."

"Not for me, you're not," I found myself saying. "I'd be delighted if you came for dinner. I'll cook you something wonderful." I narrowed my eyes at her. Fuck she was sexy.

Her eyes, in return, widened and her lips clamped around her straw, as she sipped her iced cappuccino, seductively. Jesus, I felt my cock harden watching her mouth. I shifted in my seat and leaned forward to hide my bulge. As I leaned down, I let my hand brush against her golden calf. Smooth, soft legs. *Nice.* This unexpected coffee date was getting too hot to handle so I tried to turn the conversation around to stop myself from mentally undressing her. She got there first, asking me why I chose to live in New York.

"France is a great country," I began. "Beautiful. Just beautiful. Fine wine, great cuisine, incredible landscape—we really do have a rich culture. But when it comes to opportunity, especially for small businesses, it's not so easy there."

"You own a small company? What do you do?"

Interesting. This woman has no idea who I am. Refreshing. She won't be after my money—she doesn't have an agenda. Good.

"That's why I was at that conference," I explained.

I expanded a bit, gave her the usual blab about 'giving back,' and how I liked to share a few tricks of the trade with others.

"And you?" I asked, wondering what the hell this unlikely sexpot was doing at an I.T. conference. She so didn't look the type. "What were *you* doing there?"

She flushed a little, slid down into her chair as if she wanted to disappear and shifted her gaze to her feet. She looked acutely embarrassed. Maybe she had a very boring job, I reasoned, and didn't want to spoil the mood. I dropped the subject. So we brought the conversation back to me again, and she *had* heard of HookedUp, after all. Of course she had. Who hadn't? Everyone and his cousin hooked up with HookedUp, even married couples. But Pearl didn't seem particularly impressed by me, even when I let it slip that I was the CEO.

"So when you're not working or zipping about in your beautiful classic cars, or hanging out with Rex, what do you do to relax?"

"I rock-climb," I replied, already having planned in my head that rock climbing would be the perfect first date for us. Not too 'date-like,' not typical—she'd go for it.

"Oh yeah? I swim. Nearly every day. It's what keeps me sane."

Ah, so that accounts for her tight peachy ass and sculpted legs. We discussed the benefit of sports—how it was good for one's mental state of mind as well as keeping your body fit. This woman had me intrigued. I was getting more than a hard-on talking to her. She made me laugh. She was bright, opinionated. Had read the classics, loved dogs and sure, I couldn't deny it, she had a body like a pin-up and the face of an angel. Besides, with all her straw-sucking, I knew what was going through her mind. She wanted to see me with my shirt off. Yes, damn it, I could tell. She couldn't take her eyes off my chest. She even licked her luscious lips while she was ogling me, and then said—her eyes all baby-doll…all come-and-fuck-me-now:

"I tried rock climbing once. I was terrified but I could really understand the attraction to the sport."

On the word, *attraction*, I swear to God, she looked at my chest, then my groin, and back again to my chest before she finally fastened her gaze on my face. Oh yeah, believe me, I knew what was going on in Pearl's mind. Her smart attire, educated voice and expensive handbag didn't fool me. Still, her come-on would have been imperceptible to an un-trained eye—not slutty, not over-flirtatious…just a split second of wanton lust on her part, which I bet she thought I hadn't clocked onto.

But…Miss Pearl Robinson, daughter of hippies, lover of dogs, quasi-vegetarian temptress….I had your number.

I knew everything there was to know—instinctively.

I wanted her quirky ass and I was going to have it. And everything that went with it, too. All of it. I was going to put my mark on that peachy butt.

I presumed I had her all worked out. Clever me.

Little did I know that I was dead wrong.

Things weren't going to be quite so simple.

2

So there we were chatting about this and that, still drinking our coffees, lingering over them, trying to make our drinks last, because neither of us wanted our tête-à-tête to end.

During the conversation that followed, it struck me that Pearl was damaged goods. But it was too late. *I was invested.* I invited her rock climbing—feeling smug about all the things I was going to do to her, picturing her having multiple orgasms as I fucked her senseless in several different ways. How I'd take her to a hotel the night before, we'd have passionate sex, and by the next day, she probably wouldn't even want to go rock climbing anyway, because let's face it, when she told me she'd once been, she was obviously lying.

"Would it seem too forward to invite you to come with me for the weekend?" I suggested.

Her eyes lit up, *at first,* "Not at all!" she said with enthusiasm. But suddenly, she froze. *Froze.* She was like a beautiful flower closing its petals. I saw horror flash across her face. She was even eyeing the front door as if she planned to make a dash for it. Why? She was stunning, had a great body (so must have felt confident in that department), fancied the pants off me, obviously wasn't playing the hard-to-get-I'm-so-virtuous game, so why was she freaking out about us spending the night together?

I read her expression: she was terrified of sex.

"Don't worry, Pearl. I can arrange for us to have separate bedrooms," I said.

But it only made things worse: she looked even more panicked; her face paled, her mouth fell open. She mumbled—her disappointment deeper than a well, "Yes, of course. Separate bedrooms."

I understood, then and there, that she wanted me, but would be too traumatized for anything more than a peck on the cheek.

How did I know all this at the tender age of twenty-five? I won't go into it now, but trust me, I know women. I've been intimate with the female species—because they *are* a 'species' unto their own—since the age of fourteen, when I lost my virginity to a friend of my sister's, a 'colleague' of hers. Women have always revealed to me their deepest secrets, fears, loves and passions. How many women have I 'known' in my life? I lost count a long, long time ago. Because I started young, by the time I was college age, I really was *au fait* with the physical and physiological machinations of the female sex. Not that I went to college. Not for long, anyway. I was too busy plotting to take over the world, shut in my man cave. Coding. Being a nerd. Designing HookedUp. But as most people know, nerds get their revenge. One day I'd be a rich man, I told myself.

And I was right.

So by the time I was the grand old age of twenty, I'd played the field so much that all I wanted was a safe, stable relationship with a normal girl. I ended up in the arms of someone less than stable and swore I wouldn't make the same mistake twice. But here I was again, being drawn to somebody with *issues. Major issues,* I suspected.

And that somebody was Pearl Robinson.

I was a rich, powerful man used to getting what I wanted. And ironically, I wanted her.

So I suggested I'd pick her up the following day. No hotel. I'd play it safe.

"Actually, I know another place that we can go rock climbing closer to the city. It's only ninety miles upstate—we can drive there early and come back late, all in one day. What do you say?"

"Great," she answered. And I saw both relief and regret flicker in her blue eyes.

I wouldn't fuck her, after all. I'd wait. Bide my time. Because something told me that this woman hadn't been fucked properly for a very long while. Maybe never.

Most guys like the chase. They love it when girls spurn them and play hard to get. I guess they have something to prove to themselves, like going hunting. But I don't operate that way. I don't want a woman to be with me because of my own powers of persuasion, or because I've 'bulldozed' her into it. I'm not the bulldozing type. I don't want to tread over anyone's sensibilities, least of all a female's. You know how children and dogs can be? Curious but wary? You can't force them. Let them come to you, I say. Pique their interest. Don't be overbearing or over-possessive.

It makes for a good story in a romance novel (I know, my mother devours them, one a day), but in reality, a woman wants a man to be a man, not some insecure wreck wondering where she is every second, or having a jealous fit if her top's too revealing. A woman desires a *confident* man—that's another thing I've learned over the years from listening to their woes: be confident.

And if you aren't feeling that way?

Fake it.

Besides, I believe in love at first sight, or at least, *lust* at first sight. If the magic isn't there for both parties within the first twenty seconds of meeting each other, you can be sure it never will be. Of course, many people would disagree with that, but for me, I've found this to be true. With Pearl that connection was there. Has it ever been there before or since? No, never. Not in that twenty-second kind of way.

I didn't let Pearl know how I felt. Another rule: Don't scare a woman off by being too keen or pushy. Because if she succumbs to you, you'll never know if it's because she genuinely loves you or because you've worn her down. There are a lot of worn-down women out there. They think it's easier to give in. Some men are foolish enough to mistake that for lust, or even love.

Also, I'm French. Pride is in my DNA. I can't help it. So when Pearl made it obvious that she had second thoughts about spending the night with me, I held back.

Our rock climbing date was interesting, to say the least. I picked her up at 7 am from her Upper East Side apartment, and we drove upstate to the Shawangunk Mountains. During the car ride, I knew I was giving her double messages but I couldn't help myself. One minute I was talking about falling in love with my Corvette because of the LeMans blue, adding, "Same color as your eyes," and the next I was acting like a strict Victorian father, telling her how certain types of sex play didn't do it for me—namely whipping. (Fantasy is one thing, reality is another. Seriously, what woman wants to be physically hurt?) Pearl was confused. I was confused. How the hell did the conversation veer off in that direction? Was it normal for two people to talk about sex on a first date? Talk about it, but not do it? I didn't think so, but nothing was normal about the pair of us. We were two misfits trying to slot our jiggled bits of puzzle into the right place, hoping that somehow, at least *our* pieces would fit together.

When I alluded to her LeMans blue eyes, she replied, "*My* eyes? You should talk with your tiger-green eyes set off against your dark hair."

At that point, on Date One, I wasn't quite sure what Pearl's deal was. What kind of Life Cards she'd been dealt. So far, I had learned that her hippy, surfer father abandoned her family when Pearl was young and he now lived in Hawaii. She told me that her mother died of cancer—they'd been very close. And her gay brother, Anthony (who sounded like a jerk, reading between the lines), lived in San Francisco with his boyfriend, Bruce. All this I gleaned, and yet I felt I was no closer to knowing why there was a shadow of fear in her eyes, a shimmer of benign mistrust.

Men. They can be pigs. I know, I've heard women complain about them all my life. Besides, there had been no truer hog than my father. On one of his bad days, he was a monster.

I contemplated Pearl's past. What man/men had hurt her? (Because, let's face it, it usually is a man). I studied her quietly all day. While she was climbing, she was brave and very focused. Even though she had never been rock climbing before, she embraced that rock-face with gusto. I got to enjoy great views of her slender legs doing their stuff, her nimble fingers hooking into tiny crevices, her glorious ass in all sorts of uncompromising positions. I heard myself calling her *chérie* and that's when I knew that I must have wanted to date her seriously. Chérie? I had never called *anyone* that before, not even my ex fiancée, Laura.

"You've passed the second test," I teased on the drive back home. My 1968 Corvette was humming away beautifully, and I didn't want Pearl to fall asleep. I saw exhaustion in her eyes after such a long, physical day. Her golden legs were stretched out, scratched by the rocks; there were little bloody nicks all over her limbs. I liked that. I may not have fucked her yet, or even kissed her, but I felt I'd made my mark on her. Yes, just like the bull-dozer guys, I was guilty. Even on Date One, I wanted others to know that Pearl Robinson was mine.

She jolted from her sleepy reverie and shifted her weight in the car seat. "Second test? I didn't know I was being tested!" She laughed. "I'm assuming going climbing was the second test. What was the first test, then?"

"You have no idea?" I said, thinking it was obvious after our detailed conversation about Rex and Zelda, and dogs in general. Actually, come to think of it, this wasn't Date One but Date 1.5. We'd been through all the preliminaries in the coffee shop. Had she turned her nose up at the mention of Rex, it would have been an instant deal breaker. I didn't, and don't, trust people who are not animal lovers. *Must love dogs.* No ifs or buts about it. I'd made that mistake once before.

"Go on, give me a clue," Pearl pleaded, raising her legs onto my dashboard, her bare feet revealing perfect, slender toes, set off by delicate ankles. I wanted to suck those pretty toes, then move my mouth further northward up her body.

"Give me a hint," she said with a pout. That pouting mouth. *Very sexy!* I had not-so-pure visions of things I wanted to do to that mouth, and things I wanted *it* to do to me.

I said nothing, just gave a cocky little smirk. I wanted to intrigue her, make her think about me. Dream about me when she got home that night. Make her want me. I could tell that, so far, it was working. I changed the music…*Can't Get Enough of Your Love Baby* by Barry White—a sexy song with a rhythmical drum beat. It set the scene. She jiggled about in her seat and I was curious. I wanted to know if she was moist between her legs. I wanted to know, for sure, if she was feeling as horny as I was.

I put my hand on her bare thigh and let it rest there, tapping my finger *very* lightly to the beat of the music. She whimpered. Very, very quietly. Almost imperceptibly but I caught it. I had her. But I still wouldn't fuck her that night. No, I'd make her wait. Make her wonder. I let my fingers wander higher. I had my eyes on the road, but in my peripheral vision, I noticed she licked her lips and fluttered her eyelashes. So very subtly, I let my fingers creep closer to her panties. I could sense her chest heaving with hot desire. Her nipples were erect—I saw that through her skimpy outfit. *Good,* I thought. I so wanted to plunge my fingers inside her, but instead, I took my hand away and put it back on the steering wheel. She sighed with frustration. I was getting to her—getting under her skin.

3

My cell had been switched off all day; I didn't want any interruptions. I had ten messages on my voicemail, more than half of which were from various women in my life: three from Sophie, all business calls except the last—she was curious as to where I'd been all day, and wondered who the lucky woman was. It seemed that it was my karma to attract jealous women, even my *sister* was possessive of me, and that's one of the reasons Pearl appeared so different; she was vaguely aloof, even though I could tell she liked me.

The next calls were from Laura, my ex, telling me that she would be coming to my house in Provence. I listened to the messages with half an ear, her Queen's English more pronounced than ever.

"Hi Alex, darling. Just to say that my plans have changed a bit. James doesn't seem to want to come this year, so it'll just be little old me. Is that okay? Of course it's okay. But I'll be really miffed if you're not there at the same time. I mean, I'll get bored all alone. Speak later, Alex, darling."

Then another:

"Oh yes, I almost forgot, just to let you know my physiotherapy sessions are going really well. I mean *really* well. I haven't been using the wheelchair for six whole months now. I'm a bit wobbly still, but it's all looking good. I mean, *I'm* looking good, though I say it myself! Call me, darling, and let me know when you'll be in France and I'll make plans."

If Laura said she was looking good, I believed her. She had been a model once, before she had a nasty accident with some concrete steps and ended up in a wheelchair. She had been a sailor, too—practically Olympic standard. Why I felt that the accident was somehow my responsibility, I don't know. But I did. Guilt has a way of grabbing you by the throat. Hence, my unfounded belief that I was responsible for Laura's happiness, despite her being married to another man.

The next message was from Indira, the woman I was fucking. I'd be seeing her the following week in Mumbai. Her Indian accent was husky and breathy, laced with desperation and desire.

"Baby, I can't wait to see you. I'm going crazy. Crazy, I tell you. I can't wait to lie with you. I've been dreaming of you every night. I need you so badly. See you next week."

Lie with you. What a quaint, polite way of saying, 'fuck.'

Indira was a movie star. A Bollywood legend, even though she was only thirty-three. She had long, dark, wavy hair and pale gray eyes, set against her caramel-colored skin. Stunning. She was a real beauty, gracing magazine covers and cherry-picking leading roles. She was also a widow. Her husband had died a few years before, leaving her a small fortune, not that she needed it—she was wealthy in her own right. He'd been a film producer, and was a good thirty years older than Indira. She had one grown-up teenager who was also making her name in movies. Women in India were generally treated like second-class citizens, except in two key areas where they really had clout: politics and cinema. Indira was a powerful woman, and used to getting what she wanted.

And she wanted me. Or rather, she wanted my cock.

I needed to end it with Indira but it was going to be tricky, because the grease-ball bastard with whom Sophie and I were signing our upcoming deal, was her first cousin. Indira was also investing a large chunk of her own money into HookedUp in India. Something I begged her not to do—I never mix business with pleasure—but she was insistent, and Sophie would have never forgiven me if I'd bungled the deal.

Meanwhile, I had Pearl Robinson on my mind.

Hmm…could get complicated. With Pearl Robinson now on the horizon, I wasn't sure how I'd organize my time. It depended on Pearl, really. Would she want me as a full-time boyfriend? I assumed so. Another thing I'd learned about women over the years: the exclusivity factor. Even Laura, who was married to someone else, wanted exclusivity. Not that I was fucking Laura, but I got the feeling from her flirtatious demeanor, that she was keen for our old candle to be re-lit.

The last voicemail was from Claudine. An ex from my teenage years. Uh oh. I'd be seeing her the next day. Now, Claudine was so fucked-up, that to *not* see her could be dangerous. I really didn't want a suicide on my conscience.

I listened to the message: "Alex? Mon amour?" She talked into the receiver as if she were speaking to a live person. As if voicemails had only been invented yesterday. "Alex, tu es là?" I heard her TV on, a cackling noise in the background, her heavy breathing, as if she was waiting for me to magically say something. Then she hung up.

The last time I'd seen Claudine, she had gotten her hands on a Colt.45 and was threatening to shoot herself if I didn't fuck her. She told me that no other man could give her an orgasm. Claudine, like Laura, was a model.

Every man's fantasy seems to be to date a model, but believe me, models can be psychotic. You'd think that by being so beautiful they'd be brimming with self-confidence, but no. They can be the most neurotic women in the world. No matter how gorgeous they are, they feel they're too fat, or their forehead isn't high enough, or their lips are too thin or…whatever—the list goes on.

Claudine was like that. Very neurotic. Very high-maintenance. In order to get the gun away from her for good, I had to give her a mercy fuck. It wasn't exactly a punishment for me, but I was trying so hard to limit the complications in my life—e.g. limit the amount of women. Hone it down to just one.

I didn't consider myself a 'multi-tasker' by nature—not even when it came to women.

Quality, not quantity, was what I was aiming for.

But it was proving to be a tough call.

I was beginning to realize that my mantra of treating women well was backfiring on me.

You see I have a code:

- No woman is a 'slut'. Ever. I do not use that word in my vocabulary. If a woman is sleeping around or being promiscuous it's because she is searching: for love, for a good time, for a good orgasm, for an escape. Or maybe even for money. For whatever reason it may be, no man (or woman) has a right to judge her.
- Always call a woman after a date. Even if you never want to see her again. Why? Because it's polite. Tell her you had a nice time. Treat others as you would like to be treated yourself, especially women.
- Don't bullshit a woman. Don't say, "I'll call you," if you don't mean it. If you just want sex, make that clear from the beginning. Don't make promises you can't keep.
- Always walk her home at night, drive her home or call a cab. Pay for the cab yourself. Make sure she has unlocked her door before you drive away.
- Don't invite yourself into her house. Like a vampire, let yourself be invited.
- Don't fuck another man's girl, no matter how tempting.
- The most important rule of all: When you fuck her, let her come first.

You see, it's no good just having sex for your own pleasure. Where's the fun in that? A real man needs to know that a woman *needs* him. Even if it's for just one night, you want her remembering you for being a good fuck, not a fuck-up. Your cock is a tool that must be used carefully. As with any tool, you, the *artisan,* need to deploy it with precision. Trust me, the rewards are worth it.

Women are experts at faking orgasms and a lot of men are too dumb to tell the difference, or too proud to acknowledge that it has ever happened to them. But in that department, believe me, most women could win an Oscar.

However, having said all this, I was, at that point in my life, beginning to realize that by *not* being an asshole and caring too much, I was creating a 'backlog' of women: ex-girlfriends, and exes of every kind. It was dawning on me: *Women don't forget.* I guess there are so many assholes out there, that by being halfway decent, a man can earn big brownie points.

I'd earned too many brownie points.

And it was getting out of control.

The next day, I got up early and cadged a lift to Paris with Sophie in her jet. I had business there and wanted to drop in on my mother and see Rex. I decided that I wouldn't pick him up that time around, because of the Mumbai trip coming up, but that I'd make arrangements for him to come and live with me in New York as soon as I could. After all, he was the one I bought my huge apartment for, with its views of Central Park and its rooftop garden. Only the best for Monsieur Rex!

Sometimes, I try to imagine a world without dogs, and I can't. Rex has seen me through no end of strife. He helped me set up HookedUp. That's not a joke, it's a fact.

So Sophie and I were on the plane, about to fly to Paris. She was dressed immaculately (as always), stretching out her slim legs as she carefully tucked a tendril of dark hair into her chignon while looking into her powder compact, or whatever it is that women use. She eased herself back into her airplane seat: we were taking off. I could tell she was in 'personal' mode, not 'business' mode by the look on her face, when she began, "So you actually *like* the American?"

I frowned at her. I wasn't in the mood.

"How *is* she?" she added.

I knew what she meant by that. She wanted me to give her intimate details. I replied, "She's a very friendly, fun girl."

"Watch out."

"Why, you think she's *dangerous?"* I said with a dry smile.

"You can't risk everything by playing about with American gold-diggers."

I languidly stretched out my arms. I wasn't even going to reply to her inane comment, but found myself mumbling, "Get a life, Sophie, and stop meddling with mine."

"I'm only looking out for you."

"I can look out for myself, thanks."

"Well, when I have a moment, I'm going to get her checked out," she warned.

"Don't you dare! I hate all this Googling shit and cyber-spying. I know *we* can't talk, with *HookedUp* and stuff, but I miss the old days when you found out about someone little by little, face to face, not from the Internet. It's so bloody unromantic."

"You see *romance* on the cards with that woman?"

That woman. She sounded like Bill Clinton. I closed my eyes. "Shame you turned gay, Sophie. Because you know what? You sound frustrated. You obviously need a good seeing to."

"Oh, you think a man's penis is the answer to everything, do you, you sexist jerk."

I smirked. "You'd be surprised." *Touché.*

Sophie had a girlfriend. Fine. But Sophie was also married. Married, and with a stepdaughter, Elodie, who was eighteen. Sophie's predilection for women was a deep secret. Didn't want her husband or Elodie finding out. I had no idea whom Sophie was seeing, though. Asking my sister about her sex life didn't interest me.

"She is pretty, though—" Sophie continued, "—the American in the coffee shop. Must be in her early thirties, I'd say—a tad younger than me."

I could see that my sister was bordering on obsession.

"Very sexy. Very fuckable," she said.

"Drop it, Sophie."

"Am I right? Is she good, then?"

"I don't know."

"Ah, so she's playing hard to get, is she? Clever girl."

I put on my headphones and turned on my iPod, glad to let Al Green's *Let's Stay Together* drown out Sophie's drivel.

I always stay in the Presidential Suite at the George V when I go to Paris, and this time was no exception. My mother was disappointed, but I preferred to come and go when I pleased, not worry about offending anyone by turning up late to dinner and so forth. The hotel let me bring Rex, too—a bonus for clocking up a large bill and being such a good, repeat customer.

I was ensconced in my suite. My loyal Labrador-mix lay patiently by my side while I had various meetings with people who were keen to take a slice of the HookedUp pie. A couple of government officials dropped by; embarrassed by the fact that it had been America, not France that propelled HookedUp forward. Too late, now—they'd missed the boat for real investment.

Then, just as I was winding things up, Claudine called. I'd forgotten about her. *Christ.*

"Mon amour," she began in a sweetie voice.

"Claudine. Everything okay?" I asked, dreading what was to come.

"Look, I want to clear the air first," she said ominously. *Fuck, what did that mean?* I had a vision of her with a razorblade poised at her doll-like wrist. "I can't involve myself with you sexually anymore," she explained.

"Wow," was all I could muster. I took a deep breath. Was there a catch? *This was too good to be true!*

"I have a boyfriend now."

Poor bastard, I nearly said, but answered, "That's wonderful, Claudine."

"You're not jealous?"

"No, not at all."

"Why not?" she asked suspiciously. "Have you turned gay?"

I laughed. "I've met someone." I told her about Pearl, immediately wondering if that was a mistake. I wouldn't have put it past Claudine to stalk her, Glenn Close style.

To my surprise, she said. "I'm happy for you, I really am. Truce then? No sex, is that a deal?"

This was getting better by the second. "No sex," I agreed.

"Then I can trust you to accompany me to Delphine Aimée's *vide grenier* at her house? You won't try to seduce me or anything?"

The ego of some models, I thought, but ignored her little quip. "You're joking? *A vide grenier?*" I said. Delphine Aimée resided in one of the oldest and most beautiful mansions of Paris. She had recently died; the papers were full of her obituaries, celebrating her colorful life as one of the great Parisian beauties and fashion setters of her time.

"Her children are selling some of her furniture and belongings and I have a private invitation. A friend of a friend," Claudine went on. "You have no idea how much string-pulling I had to do to wangle this. Only a few select people are being invited to see her treasures."

"Is the house itself for sale, too?" I'd always had my eye on that mansion. A real gem. Or as the French expression goes: a rare pearl.

"If it were, it would be fifty million euros, at least."

I didn't flinch at the price. It was an old Parisian mansion and I was damned if some Russian oligarch was going to get his hands on it.

"But no," Claudine said, "the house isn't for sale, as far as I know. Just some of its contents—the family needs the money. Meet me there in an hour."

I met Claudine outside the gates of the house. She looked less pale than usual, as if she had finally had a good, hot meal. She was dressed in a pair of shorts, her long legs going on forever, her auburn hair hanging down to her waist. She looked happy, for once, less Gothic. Her dark eyes, usually coal-lined, were free of make-up.

Delphine Aimée's mansion was even more beautiful than I had remembered. It sat like a giant doll's house, not attached (a rarity in Paris), with a large garden in front, flanked by a perfectly trimmed hedge and ornate, wrought-iron railings.

The interior was no less impressive. A grand marble staircase swept up the center of the house. Above was a sort of rotunda: a dome of glass letting in streams of light, with rooms leading off a circular, balconied walkway. The floors were oak herringbone, polished to a high shine. Each room was decorated with antique furniture and great drapes that pooled on the floor in swathes of red, gold or pink damask. There were Persian rugs, and original paintings by Corot, Cézanne, and even Picasso. Delphine Aimée's daughter, a wobbly woman of eighty with a large hook nose, showed us around. She said little, just smiled and nodded, until we arrived at the great woman's bedroom. Being a man, I felt it was intrusive to enter this legend's private quarters. I stood at the doorway, but the old daughter insisted I come in. I gingerly followed her into the spacious bedroom, with high ceilings and Italian mirrors gracing the walls.

"My mother loved going to balls," she revealed in an almost inaudible whisper. "Even the most famous jewelers of her day fought to be chosen as her designers. She had the best collection of jewelry in the whole of Paris. My father was hopelessly in love with her, you know. It's always best if the man is that teensy-weensy bit more in love with his wife than the other way around, don't you agree?"

I mulled over what this woman had just said. Had I ever been *that* in love? No, I hadn't. So in love that my heart missed a beat, so in love that I thought about the other person while I breathed? It almost brought a tear to my eye just contemplating that kind of passion. Here I was, embroiled with all these different women: Claudine, Laura, Indira (and there were others, too), all wanting a piece of me, yet all I wished for was just one woman, one stable relationship, just one person who would make sense to me.

The old lady led us to her mother's dressing-table, topped with old-fashioned perfume bottles, silver hairbrush sets and miniature paintings. On top of the table, sat a black, leather jewelry box.

"Would you mind, young man, helping me with that box? It's extremely heavy. You can lay it on the bed for me."

I took the box carefully in my grip and laid it on a vast, four-poster bed. The box sank into a silk eiderdown as I laid it down.

"Some of the best pieces are in the bank vault," she told us. "The diamonds, emeralds and such. These were some of my mother's daytime choices, the ones we're willing to let go. It's somebody else's turn to give life to them. Your wife, perhaps, Monsieur Chevalier?"

She remembered my name. I was about to tell her that I wasn't married, but stopped myself. Why, I wasn't sure. Perhaps I didn't want to spoil her image of me as a happily married, family man. Because I, too, had secret longings to be a happily married family man. With children running about. Walks in the park with my beautiful wife, my little ones, and my dog. So I didn't correct the lady.

"Be my guests. Take a peek," she urged, her hooded green eyes sparkling with excitement.

"May I?" Claudine asked, taking out an elaborately carved, jade necklace.

"Of course, my dear."

Claudine looked as if she was about to pass out. "My heart's palpitating. Have you ever seen anything so exquisite in your life? And look at these earrings to match. What a gorgeous set."

"Buy it if you like it so much," I said.

"Don't be silly." And she whispered hoarsely, "Have you any idea how much this would *cost?* I'm just *window-shopping,* silly."

I suddenly felt ashamed. This kind old lady was opening up her museum of a house to us, her *heart* to us, and Claudine was admitting to just *window-shopping?* I knew I had to do something. Fast.

"I'd love to buy something," I said, glaring at Claudine. I turned to the lady. "What else do you have?"

"What's your wife's name?" the eighty-year-old asked.

I hesitated. I've never been fond of lying, but not putting the facts straight wasn't a *lie* exactly… just a little…*white* lie. "Her name is Pearl," I blurted out without even thinking, and in that second, crazy as it sounds, I had another premonition—one day, Pearl, would indeed, be my wife.

The lady grinned, her wrinkly mouth revealing a naughty yellow fang, and she said, "I have just the piece for you, Monsieur." She shuffled back to the dressing table and opened a drawer. She brought out a pale blue leather box which was scuffed and had seen better days, but still, was obviously once from one of the best jewelry houses in Paris. "This is from one of the jeweler's in La Place Vendôme," the lady said. "Open it."

I carefully opened the box. Inside, was an unusual-looking, double-strand of pearls. The pearls graduated subtly in size. It was more a choker than a necklace, with a diamond and platinum, Art Deco-style clasp. It was beautiful. I had a flash of it around Pearl's elegant neck, her blonde hair setting off the golden-pink, honey-colored pearls. I had just planned on getting Pearl some little thing, just a token gift from Paris—I didn't want to come on too strong—but the second I saw the choker, I knew that it had Pearl's name written all over it. *Pearls for Pearl.* Perfect. "I'll take it," I said without hesitating.

"It will be expensive, Monsieur," she warned.

"I don't care about the price, I'd like to buy it, please. If that's alright with you, of course, madame."

"My father had them especially designed for my mother. It was her wedding present. There are eighty-eight pearls. They brought her good luck whenever she wore them."

"Eighty-eight is a lucky number," I said. "The number of infinity, the double directions of the infinity of the Universe, the period of revolution—the days it takes for Mercury to travel around the sun." *Only a nerd can know these things.* I smiled to myself, wryly, thinking back to my schoolboy years when I spent hours reading the encyclopedia, memorizing whole chunks by heart of facts that interested me.

"It's the number of keys on a piano, too," the woman replied. "My mother played so, so beautifully."

"It's an untouchable number," Claudine added. "Whoever this Pearl chick is, I'm envious of her. She's gonna flip out when she sees that choker."

4

But Pearl didn't flip out. She didn't even call. I'd had the pearl choker delivered by hand to her apartment; the box within another box, within a huge box with her name on it. It couldn't have gone missing. Nothing. No reply. Not a word.

I began to ponder the reason for her silence. My interest was piqued. It should have been a warning sign, telling me, *She's an ungrateful, ill-mannered brat.* But it made me wonder about her. Did she have a boyfriend? Worse, maybe, *she was married.* Shit, that possibility hadn't occurred to me. *The husband was probably having a jealous fit!* Maybe, he'd found the box first and chucked it away. *Fuck, I should have thought of that.* Duh! On our date and at the coffee shop, I had never actually ascertained whether Pearl Robinson was attached!

My mind flipped back to all our conversations. Yes, I remembered her asking *me* if I had a girlfriend. But did I ask *her* if she had a boyfriend or husband? NO, I DID NOT!

It was obvious by that point. This woman, whom I was fantasizing about, was bloody well married!

That's why she freaked out about spending the night at a hotel with me! *That's* why she looked terrified of having sex. A little flirtation, fine. But cheating on her husband? It obviously wasn't her style. He must have been out of town on business and she was up for having a little fun. That's why she accepted going on a date. My mind wandered back again to our conversations. I did remember asking her about her family and she didn't mention a husband, but had I asked her directly, *Are you single?* No, I had not!

I thought of one of my golden rules: *Don't fuck another man's girl.* I felt like a fucking idiot.

By the time a week had gone by, piqued interest had morphed into near obsession. I should have called, should have just said, *Hey, Pearl, did you get the necklace?* But my pride got the better of me.

I couldn't get her out of my mind. Her ass. Her pert breasts which I'd noticed through her light, summertime dress. Just thinking about her was giving me a hard-on. Why hadn't she called me? She had my business card—I'm sure I'd given it to her. Hadn't I?

All these thoughts were spinning about my head. I was trying to concentrate on work, but all I could do was think about fucking Pearl Robinson.

So by the time, one whole week later, I got a message from her on my voice-mail, saying 'thank you' and apologizing for taking so long about it (the doorman had apparently forgotten to give her the box), my dick was behaving as if it had a brain of its own and propelled me to get in a cab and head straight over to her apartment. If she wasn't single, I told myself, I'd soon find out. Her apartment would give me instant clues.

If she was attached, I'd walk away.

But if she wasn't, I'd fuck her.

I took a risk and bought champagne and flowers. If I was greeted by the husband....

Well, I'd have to cross that bridge when I came to it.

The doorman opened the door for me and I sauntered into the lobby, trying to look casual but realizing that I was feeling edgy. I gripped the chilled bottle of Dom Pérignon in my hand and tightly held the bunch of roses I'd bought.

"Good evening sir," the uniformed doorman said.

"Good evening. Pearl Robinson, please."

"Ah, Mrs. Robinson," he replied with a knowing smile.

Mrs? Fuck! So *she is bloody married,* I mumbled to my dick, which had been, up until now, *so* cocky, *so* confident that he was going to score. "*Mrs.* Robinson?" I repeated.

"Mrs. Robinson is upstairs, sir."

"Is her husband in?" I asked weakly.

"Husband?"

"Yes, her husband." My dick was seriously disappointed. I felt like a fucking fool standing there with flowers and a bottle of Dom Pérignon.

"No, no husband," the doorman answered, his thick moustache twitching above his inanely happy grin.

"But she is *Mrs.* Robinson?"

"She *was* Mrs. Robinson, now she's Mzzzz. Robinson," the doorman replied, still smiling. "She is a very modern woman. I call her now."

The Ms. Made me feel more relaxed. Although, a lot of American women prefer Ms. even if they are married so that was no guarantee. Or, if not married, Ms. meant Pearl could be dating on a regular basis. But I figured that if Pearl was busy, otherwise occupied with another man, she'd tell me to piss off.

I waited, trying to look patient while the doorman called on the landline.

"No answer," he told me.

"But you say she's in?"

"Yes, she's definitely at home."

I realized that I was about to be just as guilty as the 'bulldozer' types I despised. I wanted Pearl Robinson and I wasn't going to let this go. I called her myself, on my cell.

She finally picked up. "Yes?"

"I'm downstairs," I said, forgetting to say who I even was.

"I'm in the bathtub," she replied.

And my dick (because I swear it wasn't me) answered, "Good, I'll join you."

"Pass me onto Dervis, the doorman," she said.

Uh oh. This is the moment that she's about to get me flung out of the building.

Dervis listened, nodded, smiled into the receiver and said, "Okay, Mrs. Robinson."

So it *was* ***Mrs.*** Robinson, after all. I turned on my heel to go, but the doorman shouted after me, "Mrs. Robinson's expecting you. You can go up." He buzzed open the elevator door for me and pressed the button for her floor. "Enjoy your evening, sir," he said, beaming.

When Pearl opened the door, my heart missed a beat. *Fuck!* She was wearing the choker, and all she had on was a towel draped about her hot, sexy body. She had just gotten out of the tub and smelled like heaven, sweet and tender and…*Jesus.* She looked so gorgeous, so fucking fuckable. Her eye make-up was slightly smudged, giving her a sleepy, bedroom look. I could feel my cock expand in my jeans. I *had* to have her. Right there, right then. Mrs. or Ms. I didn't care, I'd have to break my code, if need be. Pearl Robinson was going to get my attention that very night.

I moved in on her like the bulldozer I was morphing into. "I've missed you, Pearl," I said, putting down the champagne and flowers on the hall table.

Her mouth opened and her eyelids started fluttering. Sex was so thick in the air that neither of us could hardly breathe. "You're wearing the necklace," I said, raking my eyes down her body, knowing that I was about to rip that towel off her.

"The necklace is stunning," she whispered, then caught her bottom lip between her teeth.

She started protesting about how she shouldn't accept such a gift. Women always do that. They don't want you to believe they're greedy but they have no intention of *not* accepting your gift. Pearl was no different. I saved her by saying something like:

"That necklace was made for you, Pearl. Nobody else has the right to wear it." Did I tell her that she was beautiful? I must have, because she did look incredible. Like a classical painting.

Elegant, even half-naked. Poised, even though wanton.

I couldn't stop myself. My cock was on fire. I pushed her up against the wall, right there by the elevator door, and start licking her lips slowly, softly. She moaned. I growled like a beast, ripping that towel off her, as I probed her mouth with my tongue, kissing her deeply, passionately.

"Fuck, you're beautiful," I murmured into her mouth, and I meant every word. She closed her big blue eyes and yielded to me completely, returning the kiss with everything she had. I let my mouth wander down to her neck as my lips brushed softly over her sweet skin. The choker accentuated every delicate curve, every tiny muscle. I noticed how she swallowed as if she was about to drown in her own desire.

My tongue traced across her collarbone, down her chest, to her tits. Her beautiful, pert tits that turned upwards, but were full and hard. I slid my tongue over to one nipple, swirling it around till her rosebud turned taut, and I sucked greedily. I groaned again and grazed my fingers down the crack of her butt, trailing them further down between her thighs. She was soaking wet. Already, and I'd hardly even begun. I could feel her nails in my back, then clawing softly across my biceps, they made their way over my pecs and the muscled ridges of my abdomen. Her touch was driving me crazy. She cupped my huge, throbbing cock through my jeans.

"Not yet," I said. "Ladies first."

She splayed her legs apart a touch, thrust her hips forward, trailed her hands from my back, up the nape of my neck and then dug her fingers into my hair.

"Fuck, baby, I'm going to have to do all sorts of things to

you," I whispered in her ear, before nipping her gently on her lobe, then along her jawline. She shuddered. I was burning with unprecedented desire, every cell in my body awakened. Her skin was so soft and unblemished and she smelled like an exotic flower. I breathed her in, ran my thumb over her full lips, taking a moment to appreciate all that was before me. *Sugar and spice and all things nice.* I remember thinking, in that second, how women really were the best invention. Ever. God must have been particularly inspired on that extremely creative day.

I palmed her pussy with one hand and slipped a finger inside her. Her hot flesh was deliciously slick. "You're really asking for it, aren't you, Pearl Robinson?"

She said nothing, just whimpered and circled her hips. She was so ready to be fucked by me, but I'd make her wait. Make her beg for it.

"Ooh, chérie, so perfect, so wet," I said, spinning her around so her ass was up against me. That peachy round ass that was doing things to my brain. I felt it press against my groin; my erection was screaming at me to fuck her, right there. Pound into her, hard. Push her down on the floor and fuck her senseless. But I needed to control myself. With one hand, I rolled her hardened nipple between my fingers, and with the other, I slipped my thumb inside her, with all my fingers cupping her mound, tautly. I had her, all of her, in my contained grip.

"So juicy, so designed for me," I rumbled into the nape of her neck. I could feel the swell of her wet clit, hard and pulsating. So ready for me. I was driving her to distraction but I wanted her to be totally and utterly relaxed, so I said, "Let's have some champagne, shall we?"

With my other hand I grabbed the champagne and flowers from where I'd set them on the hall table, earlier. I steered her forward while I walked behind her, my thumb still inside, her pussy all mine in my hand, while I simultaneously massaged her clit, her moisture hot on my fingers. I loved it. This woman was mine. All fucking mine. After a little while, I took my hand away, trailing a finger up her butt crack again, and letting my hand rest on the small of her back.

I said, "Come on. Champagne time. We need a drink. The flowers also need a drink."

I was still fully dressed. She was nude, with only the pearls about her pretty neck. The whole scenario made me feel amused. And very in control. Pearl was utterly undone.

She spun around to face me. "Is this what you always do, Alexandre Chevalier? *Manhandle* women like this? You were holding me like a six-pack!"

"But you loved it," I said, getting down on my knees. I whispered light kisses on her taut belly and flickered my tongue downwards. I could feel her quivering as I nuzzled my head in between her thighs. She gasped. I rested my tongue quietly on her clit and she pushed herself closer with a moan. I licked her in great sweeps and tasted her honeyed juices as I explored her wetness with my tongue. She tasted delicious, her sweet nectar making me so fucking hard it was almost painful. Hot. Welcoming.

"Sexy little pearlette," I mumbled into her pussy, coining a new word that suited her perfectly; fucking her with my tongue, flicking it on and around her sensitive nub. *My Pearl and her little pearlette.* Pearl was groaning out loud. As for my part, this was giving me so much pleasure, I was literally about to come myself.

"Oh, God," she murmured, fisting and clawing her hands in my mussed-up hair. "This feels incredible."

But I taunted her again. Stopped what I was doing and led her to the kitchen. She got up onto a chair to retrieve some champagne glasses from a cupboard. They were vintage, crystal ones, the kind you didn't often see anymore. She mentioned that they were a wedding present from her mother and I realized that, *oh shit*, I *was* fooling around with a married woman, after all. I decided that, as long as I didn't actually penetrate her, I could get away with this.

My rule was, *Don't fuck another guy's girl,* not, *Don't play around with another guy's girl.*

I made excuses for myself.

I liked having her up on that chair. She was vulnerable and couldn't escape from me. She had the delicate glasses in her hands so her wrists were as good as bound, because she didn't want the glasses to drop. I held her hips still so she couldn't move. I began with her ass—what was it about that ass that had me so fucking mesmerized? The fact that it was round and firm? Maybe. Whatever…I was transfixed. And hard as a fucking diamond.

I started licking up and down her butt crack, something I never usually did to women. But Pearl had me drooling for her like a horny devil. I could feel her ease herself into the situation, her body heaving with yearning desire. I looked up and noticed her erect nipples as I controlled her hips with both my hands. I pressed the small of her back forward so she was bending over slightly, slid my thumb inside her wet warmth and located the magic spot that I knew would drive her wild. My thumb pressed this erogenous zone while I circled her clit with my palm. I went back to licking her butt crack again. Slowly. Deliberately. Up. And then down. Up. And then down. I could feel her center throbbing. She was panting and thrusting, and pumping her clit hard against my firm hand.

"Alexandre!" she screamed "Oh, sweet Jesus, what are you doing to me?"

I probed my tongue into her sweet ass, tunneling deep inside, flicking and licking. She was all clean and fresh, oiled up from her bath. She smelled of orange blossom or vanilla, or something that sent my head spinning. Simultaneously, my fingers continued the rhythmical massage on her clit, my thumb still circling inside her. She couldn't take it anymore—she was about to detonate. I could hear her screaming while she contracted around my large thumb, her orgasm coming in a hot rush. "Oh, my God! It's like triple pleasure….oh fuck….I'm coming," she yelled out, still gyrating against my hand. "I'm coming so deep…so deep from inside!" She sounded shocked, surprised as hell.

Was *I* surprised?

Not one bit. I knew exactly what I was doing. I'd zapped her G-spot. Hit the jackpot.

And this was just the beginning.
The beginning of something beautiful.
Something inevitable.

5

I never did get to fuck Pearl that night, but I did learn all about her. Well, about her sexuality, anyway. While we were drinking the champagne, I asked her about her first orgasm. She was lying seductively on her chaise-longue in the living room, wearing nothing but my shirt, while I stroked her long, lean legs, kissed her, licked her, and generally absorbed the wonder of her, letting her very being seep into my every pore. She struck me as so intrinsically beautiful, not just physically, but there was a sweetness about her, an innocence, as if she was completely unaware of her splendor. Even though she was blonde, her lashes were thick and dark and her skin a sun-kissed gold. She was a genuine, star-spangled, American girl. Wholesome but elegant. All in one, sexy, very fuckable package.

I caressed her gently, enjoying her softness, the delicacy of her smooth skin, while she revealed to me that she couldn't come from penetrative sex; at least hadn't since she was twenty-two, when she dated her best friend's brother. It seemed as if all this time she had been alone, although I finally asked her *the question,* which I had been avoiding, probably because I was nervous of the answer.

"Pearl, this may come as a stupid question….a little late, I know, but—"

"What?"

"You mentioned that those crystal glasses were a wedding gift, and your doorman calls you *Mrs.* Robinson. Are you *married,* by any chance?"

She laughed. "You think I'd be lying here, now, in this uncompromising position if I were married?"

I shrugged my shoulders. "Maybe."

"No, that's not my style. I *was* married but got divorced a couple of years ago."

I could hear my lungs heave out a sigh of relief.

That's when, I guess, most men would have fucked her. And yes, I was tempted. Of course I was.

But I wanted to wait. Why? Because I realized that I was dealing with a neo-virgin. A woman who hadn't had an orgasm with anyone in all those years? I'd need to take it slow, I decided. Make her first time with me special. Something she'd never forget.

As she lay there, slightly tipsy, she said, "Really, Alexandre, I'm too much of a head-case. You should be with someone much younger than me. Someone more receptive."

I thought she was kidding. She was the most receptive woman I had been with in ages. She was honest, vulnerable. When she came, I thought she might collapse she seemed so affected. I didn't want some sassy college girl who'd experienced very little of the world, who'd never had any real knocks or bruises to call her own. I needed, I understood in that moment, a damaged bird. I wanted to repair her wing and help her fly again. Set her free. Hope that she would fly back to me of her own accord.

Pearl was that bird with the broken wing.

The more she tried to convince me that I was wasting my time even trying with her, the more I was determined to fix her.

She stroked me tenderly on the cheek. "I don't want you to be disappointed with me, Alexandre. I can't come with sex, not even oral sex. I haven't been able to for years. You're gorgeous and everything but—"

"There are no buts, chérie," I told her. "An orgasm isn't just physical. It's all about your mental state of mind. The biggest sex organ of all is your brain. Think of the Big O as an orchestra that needs a conductor. I want to be that conductor, to conduct sweet, mind-blowing music that climaxes....right—" I trailed my finger down her stomach over her mound of Venus and tapped her gently between her legs—"here," I said.

She closed her eyes blissfully but shook her head as if to say that what I was describing was impossible.

But impossible is not a word in my vocabulary.

I had a mission:

To be the best fuck that Pearl Robinson had ever had in her life.

6

I was still thinking about Pearl while I navigated my way around the capital city of Mumbai. It was hot and sticky. Traffic everywhere. The streets were seething with ramshackled activity: cows dodging rickshaws (because cows are holy in India so they hang out, loose on the streets), scooters, diesel-belching trucks, cars, all ebbing and flowing as people tried to cross jam-packed roads without getting mowed down. Although India was still a third world country, it was innovative and ahead when it came to I.T. Not to mention the sheer volume of inhabitants. That's why Sophie and I were keen to establish HookedUp there. But it was proving to be less than straightforward because of government corruption. So we decided that the best approach was to keep ourselves out of running the show in India. Sell them our company's franchise and let them deal with it. There was no way either of us wanted to get embroiled in the day-to-day bribery and fraud that was an evil necessity there.

We'd take the money and run, so to speak.

Not in cash. But in precious stones and gems.

Sophie and I had several specialists on our team because we didn't trust a soul. Especially, the baggy, boozy-eyed bastard who was procuring the gems: Indira's cousin.

Indira…

I was on my way to see her. We'd always meet at the Leela Hotel: a lavish, five-star piece of heaven that sits on the outskirts of the city, amidst the chaos that is Mumbai. We'd spend a relaxed day together swimming in the pool, having massages or a long lunch, although in India you can never feel completely at ease, knowing how the other half live; one-armed beggars, hungry children and mangy, half-starved dogs. Living beings that make you feel guilty with all you own, yet their problems are so bottomless you don't know where to begin.

Don't get me wrong; there's magic in India, too. Real beauty. But every time I visit, it always takes a while to adjust to its inequality: the uber-rich and dirt-poor living side by side.

I had employed Indira to set up a charity for me in Mumbai. That's how we became acquainted in the first place. Being such a high-profile star, she could garner lots of interest and attention. She'd done an amazing job, so far. I admired her for her tenacity. She had gathered a lot of other Bollywood actors on the board of directors, and they were doing so much good. But I wanted to pull out completely. I was keen to extricate myself and let her get on with it herself, without me.

The charity was for children and their education. It incorporated schools and means for training them for professions where they could get real jobs. It was very hands-on, and the Bollywood stars made personal appearances every month or so. That made the kids turn up, because they were fearful of missing out on the action. Attendance was great. Movie stars have so much power in India—even more so than in the USA.

Indira was lying on the bed in the hotel, waiting for me. Red rose petals led like a carpet from the door to the bed, sprinkled about like confetti, spelling out our names and arranged in the form of hearts. She had a pink sari draped about her which set off her caramel-colored skin and her dark, cascading hair. I entered the room and gazed at her. She was stunning, no doubt, but there was someone else who had taken precedence. Someone else who had stolen my attention: Pearl Robinson. As I mentioned before, multi-tasking wasn't my strong point.

"Hi baby," Indira said, batting her coal-rimmed eyes. She wore a sparkling, red *bindi* between her eyebrows and looked very exotic. She licked her lips to wet them. "Come to me. I've been so lonely. Come and lie beside me."

"You're looking good, Indira," I said. "How's it been going?" I came over to the bed, and sat down. I held her hand the way a brother or father would. She pulled me toward her and began to unravel her sari. She started to fondle her breasts, her lips parting. She cupped one hand around my groin. I could feel my cock twitch beneath my jeans. I took her hand away and clasped it again.

Alarm flashed in her gray eyes like a warning siren. "What's wrong?"

"I'm very, very tired," I lied.

But she rolled over onto her stomach, jiggled down the bed and pressed her head into my crotch. She started biting me along the ridge of my dick, through my jeans. I had to admit it was turning me on, but I wasn't in the mood to go through with it. My dick didn't agree, though. What she was doing felt really good.

She began to unbutton my pants, frantically, making mewing sounds like a cat in heat.

"I'm wet," she breathed hoarsely. "All I've been thinking about twenty-four hours a day is you. Is *this*. This beauty," she groaned, as she grappled with the material of my jeans, freeing my cock so it sprang up against her lips. I didn't have underwear on. It was too goddamn hot. I noticed how Indira hadn't kissed me on the mouth yet. It was my cock that had her obsessed. I was relieved—a kiss was the last thing on my mind—too intimate.

"You know you have the most beautiful penis in the world," she purred between kissing and nibbling its crest. "Big, hard, thick, pulsating, en….ORmous. So thick…so huge. Proud like a cobra. So enormous…so smooth…so magnificent. It's like a work of art." She started licking her tongue up and down my erection.

I held her head still, restraining her movements. "No, Indira. This isn't a good idea."

She looked up at me from beneath her long lashes, shock flashing across her face. "Don't you fucking deny me this!" she lashed out, her mouth half full. "What the hell is wrong with you? Do you know how many men fantasize about me doing this to them? They dream about me while they masturbate every night, my poster on their wall. And you are telling me to *stop?*" Her large mouth stretched over my throbbing crown and she sucked hard.

I lay back, yielding to her, my dick telling me how good it felt, as if it had a brain of its own. She took my huge erection to the back of her throat, focusing on suction, greedy for it as if her life depended on it. But still, it wasn't right. It felt wrong to me. Very wrong. I forced myself to shuffle my ass away from her and sit up. My cock was throbbing with desire, but my head was telling me this all had to end.

"You're so beautiful, Indira. You're such a special lady, you really are, but I can't do this anymore. I don't want to use you, you're worth more than that." I tucked my unwieldy tackle back into my jeans.

Horror drained the color from her face. She stared at me, incredulous.

"I've met someone else, I'm sorry," I explained, getting up and going to the bathroom. I locked the door. I could hear her screaming, her abusive tirade ricocheting about the room. She was throwing things about like a small child having a tantrum. God knows who could have heard; they must have believed I was beating her up.

I had to finish off what she started. I took my cock in a tight vice of a grip and began moving it up and down ferociously. I had Pearl's hot, wet pussy in my mind's eye, her glorious ass. I was on rewind, remembering my tongue exploring all her crevices, her screams when I reached her G-spot. *Her amazing scent. Her taste. Her wet….*I clenched my cock tighter*….wet….pussy…her hot, wet, horny, tight….her mouth…her lips…her ass…her big blue eyes…her smooth skin…her wet….*I could feel myself coming hard. Semen burst from me in a thick, scalding rush. It spurted all over the bathroom mirror as my hips drove forward in one last thrust. I groaned quietly, my release felt fucking great.

As I cleaned up my mess, I could hear Indira's screeching curses. She was yelling, "Who the fuck is she? Who IS she?!" I knew I was in big trouble and I hoped it wouldn't screw things up with the charity or with her cousin.

But all I could think about was what it was going to be like when I fucked Pearl.

Actually, I didn't want to just fuck Pearl, I wanted to make love to her, too.

I called Sophie to warn her about how I'd spurned Indira and the backlash that could follow with the grease-ball cousin. My sister was quick to act. She organized a high-class sex worker to sweeten him up. The girl admitted that it was the best gig she'd ever had—she was paid handsomely for her service. Sophie, you see, used to be in the game herself. She knew about Pussy Power. I managed to steer clear of the cousin and let my sister take control of this delicate situation with Indira. But Sophie was as furious with me as Indira was. *Furious.*

On the plane back to New York, as Sophie was counting out the uncut emeralds, rubies and sapphires, her slim fingers fondling every nuance, every dimple of the precious stones—our illegal booty—she spat out:

"You fucking moron, that's the last time I bail you out, fuckhead!"

I was used to Sophie's tirades—I took them with a pinch of salt.

"What the fuck did you think you were doing snubbing such a powerful woman like Indira Kapoor?" she hissed. "Fuckwit jerk behaving like a fucking schoolboy!"

Sometimes I'd say nothing, just wait for whatever abusive adjective Sophie would come up with next. She had a good imagination. "A schoolboy would have seen the blowjob through," I said with a wry smile. "A schoolboy wouldn't have walked off halfway through, the way I did."

"A fucking dillock, wanking, fuckface fool, that's what you are!" She brought a sapphire to her lips and kissed it. I burst out laughing.

"It's not funny. Who is this silly bitch that's got you so fucking obsessed with her? What is *so special* about her? Eh? What's so great about her that you couldn't even fuck beautiful Indira Kapoor? It's that blonde, isn't it? That fucking girl-next-door?"

I took a glug of cold beer and relaxed into my airplane seat. "You said she was sexy, if I remember correctly," I goaded.

"Nobody's so sexy they have the power to jeopardize a multimillion dollar business deal."

"I don't know," I answered, thinking about a Skype-sex-session Pearl and I had enjoyed, just a while earlier. "Cleopatra stirred things up a bit."

Sophie narrowed her eyes threateningly. "Fuck off."

I'd managed to avoid Sophie earlier that day—we'd taken separate limos to Mumbai Airport, but now, I had no choice but to ride in this plane with her. I put on my headphones. This was getting to be a habit: flying about with Sophie on private jets, listening to music, in order to drown out her gibberish. I selected *Sexbomb* by Tom Jones on my iPod, closed my eyes and thought of all the things I was going to do to Pearl the second I got back. I wouldn't even go home; I'd go straight to her apartment.

7

Just rapping at Pearl's apartment door had me hard. It was about 5 a.m. She opened the door slowly, knowing it was me because I'd just phoned, but she was obviously being cautious.

"Hi," she said. There was surprise in her tone but also relief. I was hoping she'd just been dreaming about me.

She stood there in a crimson, silk satin robe. More beautiful than I remembered. Her hair was bedroom hair, wild and slept in. I went to kiss her; her mouth tasted of mint and was cool and welcoming. I ripped off her robe which shimmied to the floor, and I stepped back in order to admire her perfect body. Her legs were strong but lean, worked-out but the muscles long and elegant. I noticed her tiny waist, her feminine curves; not too slim but not an ounce of fat. Her tits were, literally, perfect. The kind any man wants to pop into his mouth and suck—ample, very full, but not too big—they didn't need a bra and the nipples lifted upwards. Pert. I had her just how I wanted her: naked.

"Come here, beauty," I whispered.

I caught both of her wrists in my right hand, pinning them behind her back. I had her captive. My other hand trailed around her breasts, circling each nipple until they stiffened. I stroked her along her neck and pulled her face to mine, cupping the back of her head. She moaned and leaned in close to me, her measured breath showing me that she was aching to be kissed.

"I've been waiting for this, Pearl. You have no idea how much," I murmured into her mouth.

I explored her curvy lips with my tongue as my erection pressed hard against her abdomen. "All I've been thinking about is all the different ways I'm going to make you come, chérie."

She opened her mouth wider and nipped me on my lower lip like a kitten. Then she fluttered her eyes as if she were in a mesmerized trance, and drew in a sharp breath to steady her nerves. I probed my tongue hard into her welcoming mouth. Greedily. Devouring her taste, my tongue lashing at hers as they tangled in a passionate dance. My hand traced down her neck to her stiff nipples as I played with each one in turn before grazing my fingers down her belly to her clit, where I rested my finger languidly. She groaned. Then I let it slide, oh so slowly, a little further, finding its way inside. As I expected, she was drenching wet. I could feel my cock swell even more. I cupped her whole core with my hand and eased my finger deep into her soaking, velvet cave. A place where I couldn't wait to call home, call my own. My dark man-cave. Because once I'd entered, I knew I'd want to return over and over again.

"I'm going to have to fuck you," I whispered in her ear. "So wet already. So. Beautifully. Wet." I thrust my finger further up inside her and felt her juices.

She was obviously enjoying the moment but was impatient for more—wanting all of me. She shook her hands free from my vice behind her back and growled like the little tigress she was. "Alexandre, let me free to do what I want—"

She went down on her knees before me and frantically unbuttoned my jeans. She ripped them down my legs and I stepped out of them. She was as hungry for this as I was. My erection slapped her in the face as it sprang free, so solid, so fucking horny for her lips. She cupped my balls in one hand and guided one into her pretty mouth. *Jesus fucking Christ!* I rocked my hips forward. It felt amazing. So hot. The thermometer was rising fast. I pulled off my shirt. My heart started racing. I gently held her head and laced my fingers through her golden mass of hair as she sucked gently on me, sending my head spinning.

"Oh Pearl. Oh Pearl, baby, you're so beautiful."

She got up from her knees to get better leverage, and bending down, started to run her lips along my shaft, teasing me, then lashing her tongue up and down along its pulsating length. I looked down at her, her lips at work with luscious concentration. Fuck this was sensual. She teased my sensitive crest, rimming the broad head round and round with the tip of her pink tongue—I swear to God, I felt it all the way down to my toes. This wasn't just turning me on, this was an *experience,* somehow different than it had been with other women. The way she was doing it with such care made me believe that there was more than just lust dancing between us. It felt as if there were molecules of love filling the air.

She looked up at me, her blue eyes full of wonder and awe

and she closed them again. Did I see a tear fall? I think so. This meant something *big* to her (didn't mean to sound crass there). But seriously, this was an intimacy that was not only electric, but strangely poetic. What she was doing meant the world to her in that moment. My pleasure was her pleasure because she was moaning while she had me in her mouth and lost in a kind of reverie.

With all the women I had been with (and there have been far, far too many) this one was different. I could tell that she was already hopelessly in love with me, and I wanted to protect her, nourish her (again, no joke intended). But I saw her as so vulnerable, my cock in her mouth as she was feasting on me. Her head was bobbing up and down and she clawed my ass with her nails, pulling me closer to her, hungry for every inch of me.

"Pearl, cherié, this is what I've been dreaming of. This feels incredible."

And I meant every word. *What I had been dreaming of.* Not just lately, but for years. Someone who was truly in *love* with me. Not only for what I could offer her, but also for what she could offer *me*. Pearl was giving me her all. Here was a woman who was no expert, but because she cared so much about pleasing me, I found it the most erotic thing in the world. She was moving fast by now, my massive length in her mouth, touching the back of her throat. She was jerking her head speedily up and down, up and down, sucking hard, her lips like a vacuum. *It felt fucking amazing.*

"Pearl. Oh you beautiful, rare pearl," I breathed, exploding as I fucked her luscious mouth, coming like a train, hard and mercilessly into her. There was a lot bursting from within me;

she'd fucking aroused me. In fact, I came twice in a row, spurting like a fountain into her sexy mouth, clamped tightly about me.

And I still wasn't finished with her. Oh no. This woman had me hooked. I wanted to see her face when I fucked her—see what she'd do when I made her come.

"That's maybe the best blowjob I've ever had in my life," I said, still tingling from all that intense pleasure, as she licked my cum from her lips.

I meant it as a compliment but Pearl looked, for just a second, as if she was about to burst into tears. I suddenly realized why. I'd basically said (in women's language): *I've fucked loads of women.* Foolishly, I used the word, 'maybe.' That was *maybe* (Jesus you have to choose your words carefully with the female sex) the best blowjob…e.g. *there's competition out there. I am comparing you with others.* Bad choice of word: maybe.

I had to dig myself out of my *faux pas*, fast.

But I couldn't help smiling. She was so sweet. So vulnerable. I pulled her up from her position and drew her close to my beating heart. I tilted her head up to me and looked into her eyes, and to reassure her I said, "Come here you gorgeous creature and give me a kiss. You know I want to make love to you, don't you?"

Her countenance changed from fear of rejection to ease. Better choice of word: *make love*, not *fuck*. There is a difference.

You see, women like the *fantasy* of being fucked. Rough. Hard. With no mercy. They even like to imagine being tied up, whipped and chastised. But in reality, they're just looking for one true thing.

And that one true thing's called *love.*

It's easy for a guy to fuck. Easy to play the rough and tough bastard that women often fall for. What's hard is to *not* be a bastard. *Not* to be a jerk.

Call me a fool, but I've always liked a challenge.

There I was, feeling on top of the world. I felt cocky and self-assured after that mind-blowing blowjob. It was obvious Pearl Robinson was crazy about me. I kissed her and she slowly, teasingly, kissed me back.

"Oh Alexandre," she groaned into my mouth.

Suddenly my tune changed. Her lips felt as if they no longer belonged to the sweet little neo-virgin who needed to be guided, but were part of a over-confident, cool, I've-fucked-a-lot-of-people-too, woman of the world. What was it? The way her tongue flickered over my top lip and made me instantly hard again, my cock throbbing for Round Two? I couldn't tell, but a jealous rage soared through my hot veins. The idea of Pearl ever having been touched by another man filled me with absolute fury. *Ridiculous!*

"Who else has fucked you before me?" *What the hell kind of question was that?* Women either lie or tell you the truth. Either way, you'll never know for sure.

She gazed at me, her look pure as a puppy. "It's been so long, I feel like a virgin," she said, her lips parting in a let-me-suck-your-cock-but-I'm-a-schoolgirl kind of way. I stared her down. Was she lying? Now I was flummoxed. I just couldn't read her.

I narrowed my eyes. "I don't believe you. The way you made me come in your mouth was too good. Too expert. Who taught you how to do that?"

"Instinct," she blurted out, her big blue eyes as innocent as a lying teenager who has just been caught with a big sack of weed.

"It's you, Alexandre. You make me want to be sexy like this."

"Who else has been fucking you?" I thought I said it in a quiet voice but it came out as a roar. I jealously sucked her tits and palmed her pussy. *Mine. All mine.* My heart slowed to a normal beat as I understood how absurd I was being. I never showed jealousy. Hell, I never even felt it. How this woman already held me so tightly under her spell after such a short time of knowing her, I couldn't fathom.

"I swear," she promised, "I haven't had sex for two years. Not since my divorce."

No sex in all that time = *tight,* I thought, and my cock got hard thinking about how I was going to be her first in so long. Divorce meant vulnerability. My cock twitched again at the thought of her needing me to care for her, protect her. For some reason that really aroused me. And if she was telling the truth about not having had an orgasm, then boy, I was going to really make her head spin.

"Good girl," I said, feeling convinced, after all, that she was telling the truth. Then I whispered in her ear, "I don't want you involved with anyone else, is that clear? I want you for myself. I'm not a jealous man but I am possessive of my treasures. You and your tight, hot pearlette are both mine, do you understand?" Choice of words, again. Not *pussy* or *cunt* or anything else that can make a woman feel like a tramp. But *pearlette.* Pearl deserved to feel treasured and loved. She'd obviously had a shit time of it in the sex department, and probably in the general male department. I could change that for her, I decided.

At the time, I would have said that I was telling her all this to put her mind at rest; let her know that I wanted to 'go steady' with her, to date exclusively. But the truth was that I was scared for the first time in my life when it came to the opposite sex. I was scared of losing her.

Because, God damn it, I realized that I was falling in love.

8

Okay, love is a very strong word. Although, lust just didn't quite cover it. Yes, I was feeling horny as the Devil himself, but I felt so much more. Yet I hardly knew Pearl. I hadn't asked her about her dreams and aspirations, whether she wanted children and a family like I did, hadn't discussed her career with her in depth. I knew nothing about her ex-husband, except for the fact he was obviously lousy in bed. I wasn't even sure how old she was, not that it mattered to me.

It felt as if I was in one of my sports cars going from 0-60 in 4.3 seconds. It was all going so ridiculously fast.

She loved dogs, she was adventurous enough to go rock climbing. She was sexy, smart, beautiful, independent, and although I very much liked what I saw, I needed to get to know her better.

I'd start by fucking her. Or rather, making love to her.

"On the bed," I ordered, leading her into the bedroom and

adding, pokerfaced, "where you belong." I'd test her sense of humor.

Her lips curled up into a subtle smile. She thought I was kidding. But I wasn't. I did want to dominate her. Control her body. But willingly. Not with whips or handcuffs, but with my sexual prowess. Make her need me, make her body lose control and have her begging for more. Give her mind-blowing orgasms, every time. I guess you could say that was pretty narcissistic but I think it was more out of insecurity on my part. I'm a pretty cocky bastard, very self-assured on the outside, but on the inside I'm just a regular guy looking for approval. I wanted Pearl to think me the hottest thing that had come along since the sauna.

"Seriously, Pearl, get on the bed. It's about time you got fucked properly."

She lay on her rather ornate, four-poster bed, nervously waiting on her back. Her breath was shallow, her breasts rising and falling, her moist folds already glistening with anticipation. I straddled her, my cock proud, rock-hard against my abdomen. I cupped her with my hand and slipped my middle finger inside her warm core, locating that sweet spot. I picked her up like a six-pack again, and she whimpered, giving herself over to me readily. I could see she had a submissive streak in her and it turned me on.

I whispered in her ear, "You really want me to fuck you, don't you?"

She could hardly speak. Just moaned and nodded her head. Her nipples were stiff, her tongue was licking lasciviously along her lips. She looked like a fucking centerfold and I wanted to plunge into her. But I had to remain focused. I lifted her up higher. She loved me taking control. I lifted that sweet pussy to my face. Her back arched and I supported her ass with both my hands. I let my tongue rest against her clit and she started bucking her hips at me. I didn't do anything—just let her feel my wet tongue pressing against her. Then I started long, sweeping strokes up and down. Up and down, along her slit. Up. And down. Slowly. Up. And down. *Oh yeah.* She tasted deliciously sweet and salty. And horny as hell; my taste buds were laced with her sexy nectar.

"Please fuck me, Alexandre. Please."

But I wanted to make her wait. Part of my plan, my history of success with the female sex: *Make women beg for it. Make them want more. Control yourself.*

I began a slow, torturous tease, fucking her with my tongue. In and out, careful not to touch her clit, which was swelling with desperation for me to play with it. Pearl was moaning, clawing her fingers in my hair, and yelling out.

"I can't take this anymore. Please. Please Alexandre, I *need* you to fuck me!"

I laid her ass back down on the bed and fished a condom out of my jeans' pocket. Lambskin. Better sensation. The only ones that fit properly and didn't pinch me. I rolled it onto my solid length. I wanted her to feel every tiny nuance, every little movement as I stretched her open. So I'd go slow. Little by little. I couldn't overwhelm her or my whole game plan would be spoiled.

I lay my naked body carefully on top of her, my erection poised at her wet entrance, throbbing and twitching a millimeter away from her. She was flexing her hips at me again; her legs open wide. Every time she pushed forward, she could feel my hardness, her clit slapping against me. She was moaning, her tongue lashing out at my mouth and I kissed her hard. Deep. Hungrily. She was getting the kiss she wanted but I wasn't going to fuck her yet, as most men would have done at that point. This took willpower, believe me.

I let myself dip into her, with tiny, shallow thrusts. Only my tip was fucking her. She was going wild.

"Oh God," she moaned. "Please, oh God. Don't stop. This is incredible."

Then I stopped. I pulled back a touch.

"Alexandre! What are you doing to me? Why are you torturing me?"

My lips flickered into a gentle smirk. "Torture can lead to heaven," I murmured. I started fucking her clit. Again, just tiny, almost imperceptible thrusts, as my hard cock massaged her between her wet folds. She was screaming. *Screaming.*

"Ssh, baby. Quiet now. So juicy. I love your hair, your soft skin, your incredible body, your Big. Blue. Eyes. On each of those words I thrust inside her, rolled in little circles to massage her clit with my pubic bone, and then pulled back out. I was huge. Swollen as fuck. I was counting in my head. *One, one thousand, two, one thousand, three*....I had to stop myself from coming. This was getting too hot to handle.

"Are you ready for all of me?" I said with a low groan.

"You're so big. It's so *huge*. Oh God!"

What she told me was the truth. What I said about your cock being a tool—that was no joke. Tools can do wonders but tools can also do damage, depending on how you use them. I had to go easy. If I pounded into her now, it would be uncomfortable for her; there was no way she'd come.

"Jesus, you're tight. Like a virgin," I said, entering her a millimeter more.

I still didn't feel she was ready to be fucked yet so I carried on teasing her with tiny thrusts, my crown feeling incredibly sensitive, even though I was wearing a condom. Then I withdrew completely, took my cock in my hand and slapped it back and forth on her hard nub. From the noises she was making and her movements, I saw she was on the verge of coming. Her eyelids started fluttering, her legs stiffened and she looked as if she was entering another zone. I pushed my cock halfway inside her and she started shuddering, her inner contractions pulsating and quivering all over me. I held it there, not even all the way in. She was moaning again, her back arched, her fingers clawing and gripping my ass like she never wanted our groins to part. Ever. She was coming hard, her hands clutching my buttocks to bring me closer.

"Alexandre, I…. Jesus, *aahh… aahh…*oh my freaking *God!*"

I stopped my *one, one thousand* and let myself go. Fuck, this girl was hot. I imploded inside my sweet, hot pearlette, luxuriating in her as we both came together, united in our carnal frenzy: our greedy, insatiable feast. "I'm coming baby, I'm coming hard," I groaned into her mouth, lashing my tongue all over her, thrusting into her with abandon at last, as my orgasm ripped right through me.

She lay there panting. Satiated. Fulfilled, with me still inside her. "I came with penetrative sex," she meowed, releasing her claws from my ass. She was shocked. Amazed. She couldn't believe what had just happened.

Was I shocked?

Not a bit. I knew what I was doing.

I started young, remember? I'd made more women come by the time I was twenty-five than most men could even fantasize about doing over an entire lifetime, even if only in their wet dreams.

9

By the time I hit my fourteenth birthday, I was already physically mature. My balls had dropped and my voice had broken to a deep baritone. I was getting tall, muscular; my Alsation roots from my mother's side of the family began to really show. Compared to other guys my age, I was pretty developed. I was masturbating constantly. All I could think of were pussies, asses and tits. But I was shy and had no intention of doing anything about my obsession.

One of Sophie's co-workers took a shine to me. She took me under her wing.

Her name was Hélène.

Sophie had been in the game since we left home when she was seventeen. But she was picky. She started out as just as an escort, refusing for a full two years to have penetrative sex. Wouldn't even blow the guys. No, she was educated, she maintained—she had more to offer. She could hold an intelligent conversation and she looked like a top model. She was ambitious, too. It wasn't long before she was the darling of several politicians and men in extremely high places. Sex was not her thing. She hooked them in a different way.

She was a Dominatrix.

They'd get off on being whipped and scolded. She'd set the scene, sometimes playing mommy, nanny or a wicked stepmother, sending them to bed with no supper or dripping hot wax onto their chests. They loved it. Some wanted golden showers. One, she even dressed up in giant diapers and spanked when he cried. It was all pretty sick but she was making a fortune. The more insane it got, the richer she became. There was one, though, who became obsessed with her. Set us up in a luxurious apartment in the Champs-Elysées, and wouldn't share Sophie with anyone. He paid handsomely for exclusivity. She became his official mistress. We were still both going under false names. She had read *The Three Musketeers* and liked the name of the author. So she chose Dumas. I was fascinated with chivalry and jousting knights so I chose Chevalier—Knight when translated into English.

We were the *Two* Musketeers, fighting to survive.

She then got bored of having to cow-tow to the politician, but before she left him, she managed to extract enough money from his coffers to set herself up in business. She became a Madame. He was furious, but her *Little Black Book* with all the names and phone numbers of some of the most powerful men in Europe spelled Doom for anyone foolish enough to mess with her. She was above the law because, guess what? She had them in her pocket: politicians, government aids, heads of police, big business men married with children, with too much at stake to lose face. Sophie was practically running Paris, not to mention her British and German contacts. She had it all sewn up very nicely.

What I later told Pearl about our stepfather helping us set up HookedUp with his piddly 15,000 euros? Bullshit. It was *Sophie* who funded HookedUp. She needed to launder money, needed to put all that cash somewhere legitimate. That's where I came in.

But back to my fourteenth birthday, several years before…

Hélène knew that I was obsessed with her. She wore black stockings, held up with garters, and a gray schoolgirl uniform. She also had a lot of powerful clients and they loved that dirty-sweet look. She was thirty but looked a lot younger. Slim, but with a curvy ass. I could smell her every time she walked by me. Vanilla, or something that smelled like candy. All I thought about was burying my cock inside her. I could hardly sleep nights I was so infatuated.

On my birthday, she knocked on my bedroom door at five in the morning. She was laughing, had been up all night and was tipsy.

She leaned back against the wall and splayed her legs apart, her high heels digging into the wooden parquet floor, her skimpy, silk panties flashing a scarlet red. "Come on then, big boy. Come and show me what you've got. I saw that huge great cock of yours bulging in your pants the other day. I have a feeling that big boy has a crush on me, doesn't it?"

I was mortified. My face was burning like a scalding iron but what she was saying was giving me a hard-on.

"You see? I just look at you and you get a stiffy." She burst out laughing again and then got down on her knees and pulled down my pajama bottoms.

When I told Pearl, "That was maybe the best blowjob I ever had," the *maybe* bit was a clue to the truth. Because Hélène's blowjob was iconic. Unforgettable.

It was my *first*. And being a green fourteen-year-old, you can imagine what it felt like.

The fuck that followed was even more incredible for me, but disastrous for Hélène. I clawed and panted and came instantly. How could I stop myself? That's when she decided I needed 'training.' I became her 'valet,' her sort of Action Man doll. She trained me, all right. She taught me almost everything I know.

After about six months, I began to get the hang of it. She wouldn't let me fuck her until she was soaking wet first. I learned to *earn* my fuck and enjoy foreplay as much as the act itself. Lubricant was banned. That was a curse word. "Any man who uses that shit isn't worth the time of day, and certainly isn't worth the time of night," she sneered. She taught me that it wasn't a race. And woe betide if I ever came before she did. Not. Allowed. Ever. If I did that, she wouldn't let me fuck her for a week.

Word got out that I had a big dick so her friends got curious and she began to share me. I was insatiable, wanting it several times a day, so I sure as hell wasn't complaining.

There were several in the game who were inorgasmic. They put on a great act, though—could have fooled anyone. And did. Fooled me, till I was shown how to read the signs: the fake screams and eye-rolls. Hélène explained that all women were natural born actresses in the bedroom, and not to be taken in by the Big Lie. They taught me how to understand women's bodies. Really know them. *Feel* them. One was even into Tantric sex, so we did it without hardly even moving. I learned to detect the tiniest twitch in her pussy and make her come by not even fucking her. Teasing her with my stillness. Making her beg for the smallest movement, which could send her over the edge. That's when I learned about the power of the brain, and that sexual organs were no more than the brain's tools.

"Don't get cocky about having a big penis," Hélène warned. "It's useless unless you know how to use it properly. God gave you a big dick for one reason only: to give us women pleasure. Don't abuse that gift. One day you'll find someone special, want to get married and have a family. The rule will still apply; you'll want to make your wife happy. If she's happy, you'll be happy. Trust me on this."

Just one woman? Marry? The idea seemed inconceivable to me at the time. I wanted every pretty woman I laid my eyes on, and that's the way it continued for many years.

But Hélène's words had an impact on me and have lived with me ever since.

Naught to sixty and I was still cruising.

I invited Pearl to dinner that very same day. To celebrate her Big O, if you like. Not that I made a big deal of it to her. I wanted her to know how special she was to me. When a woman lets a man enter her, she feels an extraordinary vulnerability afterwards, partly because so many guys start acting like assholes once they've got what they wanted. They see women as vessels for their own pleasure. That's not the way I operate. I want a woman to feel ecstatic after I have been with her, not deflated.

Besides, I couldn't get enough of Pearl.

I spent the whole afternoon preparing for her visit. I went food shopping and got gourmet treats delivered to my apartment: sea bream, hot peppers from the Pays Basque in France, black truffles, razor clams from Galicia in Spain, Cornish cream from England. I wanted to impress Pearl as much in the cuisine as I had in the sack. They say the way to a man's heart is through the stomach. Believe me, it works the other way, too. Prepare a woman a home-cooked meal and you score major brownie points.

I had conquered the business world. People needed HookedUp, or at least thought they did. It dawned on me that I liked feeling needed. Perhaps that's what came of coming from a dysfunctional family; a desire to feel accepted, needed, wanted. My mother fled when she should have stayed. She left me when I was only seven years old. So I knew all about rejection and being abandoned.

Something I still secretly feared. Yes, I wanted women—in general—to need me.

And as for Pearl? I wanted her to feel she *really* needed me.

I called Elodie, my niece, to come and help me prepare the feast. Elodie was eighteen and your typical surly teenager. However, she was bright and had an aptitude for numbers and figures so I had her working for me at the offices of HookedUp for the summer. She'd dropped out of college and was floating about, luxuriating in the fact that she was only eighteen and had all the time in the world to screw-up her life.

We stood in the kitchen, drinking cold beers, listening to Elvis Presley sing *Can't Help Falling In Love.* I had Elodie reluctantly chopping vegetables, pouting and rolling her eyes every time I asked something of her.

I raised my brows and said, "You think eighteen's young, don't you?"

She shrugged. Her dark brown hair flopped over her beautiful, heart-shaped face that was so delicate and adorable, you felt it could break.

I went on, "First kitchen rule, Elodie: hair up. Go to the bathroom and tie that horse's mane into a nice, neat ponytail or bun. I don't want strands of hair in the food."

She made a face at me. "Who is this chick that's got you into, like, Mr. Perfection mode and listening to corny love songs?"

"When you make a gourmet meal you have to pull out all the stops—get thee to the bathroom, young lady. Now!" Of course, all this conversation was in French. Elodie's English was still, at that point, floundering. I'd enrolled her in intensive classes—she needed them.

"And after this can I go to my room?" she asked, spearing a tomato.

"What? And hide behind video games, wasting your life online? No, you cannot go to your room. You stay here with me while I show you how to cook properly. Then, an hour before my guest is due to arrive, go take a shower and make yourself look pretty and presentable. Take off that dark coal around your eyes, those silly fuck-me heels that you go tottering about in, and make yourself look like a lady. There is a lady somewhere deep down inside there, isn't there? Just dying to get out?" I teased.

She jokingly wielded a large stainless-steel knife at me. "I'll go back to Paris if you keep bossing me about like this."

"What? And get driven crazy by your mother? What will you live on?"

Elodie pouted air, puckering up her lips like a model on a fashion shoot. Sophie wasn't giving her a dime. I, at least, had her on my payroll. She was learning how HookedUp operated in New York. Learning a trade. "Bathroom," I ordered. "Hair out of face. Hair out of food."

She sloped off.

"And shoulders back. Stop looking like an angry teenager and get your shit together."

I was being tough on Elodie but it was the only way to bring her out of her shell. The more I treated her with kid gloves, the more she withdrew. So I was playing dad, although she did have a real father, Sophie's husband. Sophie was Elodie's stepmother, but she had still taken her on as her own. Elodie's mom died when she was six, or so. But right now, things weren't going well between Elodie and Sophie. Elodie had clammed up and Sophie was hurting with the rejection. The usual mother/daughter stuff. I didn't ask too many questions.

Elodie thought I didn't know about her secret but I had a pretty good idea. Something bad had happened to her. Whatever it was, it wasn't pretty. It didn't seem as if it was the usual, teenage heartbreak trouble. As far as I knew, Elodie had never even had a boyfriend. No. Some shit had gone down that had broken her. Changed her from a giggly, bubbly girl into a very angry person. She looked as if she had been deceived. Destroyed. I wanted to help. I loved Elodie as my own and I felt protective towards her. To me, she felt like my flesh-and-blood daughter. I'd tried, various times, to get her to open up to me. Not easy.

Elodie clicked back into the kitchen, her hair up in a messy, ragamuffin bun. I gave her a C for effort.

"You'd be more comfortable taking off those heels," I remarked.

"I know."

"Well then?"

"I like to feel tall. Makes me feel stronger. If anyone fucks with me I can take one off and stab him in the eye."

"Ah, a weapon," I observed with a wry smile. "Interesting."

Elodie was petite. Tiny. She had wrists that looked as if you could crack them in two. Her skin was translucent, as if she had been living in a dark cave all her life. She used to be bronzed and healthy-looking, spending summers diving in and out of my pool in Provence, but now she shied away from sunlight like a vampire.

"Have you had any lunch today?" I asked her.

"An apple."

"Right. I'm going to prepare you a *steak au poivre* and French fries."

"I'm not eating meat anymore."

"No, of course not," I said, my eyes taking in the bloodless pallor of her thin skin, as I gathered some ingredients out of the fridge. "A nice, big, hearty bowl of pasta, then, with *a lot* of Parmesan on top? You need some protein, my girl."

"Whatever," she said listlessly. Then she muttered, "Who is this Pearl Robinson, anyway?"

I narrowed my eyes suspiciously. "How do you know her

name?"

"Maman mentioned her. She's getting her checked out."

I sucked in a lungful of air. "Of course she is," —and I exhaled with a long, exasperated groan— "of course she fucking is."

The dinner with Pearl went beautifully. It was the perfect date. The meal impressed her, and the delicious wines I'd chosen had her as loosened-up as a young teenager left alone at home for the very first time; innocently wicked. Her eyes sparkled; her body language spoke to me in tones of abandoned curiosity. I felt that I had her in the palm of my hand.

After dinner, we relaxed in a bath laced with lavender oil—the lavender from my very own fields. Then I played Dom, albeit with a kingfisher feather. I tied her up with some neckties of mine; her legs splayed apart, each ankle knotted to the bedpost of my big, brass bed. Her wrists I'd bound together with the pearl necklace I'd given her, which she arrived wearing, setting off a chic, black dress which was neither overtly sexy nor too smart. The sort of dress which although stunning, gives you hints to what lies beneath and invites you to rip it off as soon as you feasibly can. I surprised myself with my Dom game. It wasn't something I'd planned. It was all very spontaneous. But Pearl got off on it. She liked to be dominated. Strike that. She *loved* being dominated. And I was finding, more and more, that I liked being in control, too. Especially with her.

Mission number 2: make her come through oral sex. That was another thing I'd learned from my tutors. Don't zero in on the clitoris. It can get numb and lose all sensitivity if too much attention is paid to it. Make the clit beg. Tease it. Brush past it with light whispery kisses. Taunt it and you'll have your woman coming hard when you finally let it get its lustful way.

So I played all sorts of games with Pearl that night. I'd sent Elodie out on a date—didn't like the idea of her being in my apartment, especially as I realized Pearl was a screamer, even though my apartment was vast—still, I wanted Elodie out for the evening.

I blindfolded Pearl, dribbled honey all over her torso, smeared her tits in cream and Nutella and licked it off her curves and valleys. Her wrists remained bound as I teased her, swirling my tongue around her nipples, getting her so worked up, that by the time I pressed my tongue flat against her clit, she was ripe for a big, pounding orgasm. I didn't even have to do anything; just had to keep that pressure up and let her fuck my tongue at her own pace. She brought herself to climax, bucking her hips up and down against me. I felt triumphant, feeling her quivering quim ripple into a pulsating, tremulous orgasm right into my mouth. She was writhing about, screaming my name.

By that point, I knew she'd really fallen for me hook, line, and sinker.

Or so I thought.

A big shock was about to prove me wrong.

Pearl slept like an angel all night. The next morning, I don't know why or how, but the conversation had somehow veered itself around to my childhood. Something I never discussed with anyone. In fact, I painted it to be better than it actually was. I told Pearl that my mother returned to us a year after Sophie and I left and she stayed with my father, too chicken to come with us. But she didn't return a year later. It was *several* years later.

Pearl was shocked enough that my mother had abandoned her own son. She was less concerned about her not being there for Sophie because Sophie was my mom's stepdaughter and she was already seventeen. But I was just seven.

I let Pearl know about how my sister and I had plotted to kill my father, mixing rat poison with his food and how Sophie attacked him with a knife to his groin. After that, we had to get the hell away from him for good. My mom stayed. She was too co-dependent. Too in love. Or too browbeaten to gather the strength to leave him.

I didn't want Pearl knowing the true story; that Sophie and her sex worker friends were my real family. Still, I lay my heart open to Pearl—told her my deepest secrets. Or at least, a couple of them. Enough anyway, to be as vulnerable as a gaping wound. She, in return, told me about her brother, John, who had died ten years before of a drug overdose. I felt that Pearl and I had shared vulnerable parts of ourselves, and our jigsaw puzzle pieces were slotting together perfectly.

I was about to be proved otherwise.

We were enjoying a beautiful breakfast spread at The Carlyle. It was only 7 a.m. Pearl was wearing her elegant black dress from the night before, and high heels. She looked like a million dollars. Happy. Orgasmed-out. The way every woman should look every morning of the week. How every woman should feel.

I was spouting off a load of nonsense; something about the differences between French and American culture. Pearl was listening intently. I thought how pleasant it was that we were able to engage in interesting conversation—our relationship was not just about sex.

My cell had already buzzed a couple of times and I let it go to voicemail, but when the caller—Sophie, Claudine, Indira, Laura?—insisted, I thought that perhaps there was some kind of emergency, so I picked it up and listened to two frantic messages.

Both from Sophie.

The first:

"I was right. I knew there was something fishy about Pearl Robinson. Guess what, buddy? Your sweet little baby-doll-eyed-girlfriend is forty years old! Oh yes, fucking forty! You might be happily thinking that you are her *boyfriend* but she has other ideas: you are her TOY BOY! She's playing with you, Alexandre. She's out to get what she's after and then she'll dump you like a hot potato, you watch."

Second message:

"Sorry, forgot to explain myself. Pearl Robinson was stalking us, like the cougar she is, when we met her in that coffee shop. Coincidence, my ass! Do you remember how she pretended she just so *happened* to be there? She works for Haslit Films, the ones who were hounding us to take part in their fucking documentary! She's their producer! Do you remember that? The film company who were hassling us, wanting to do a piece about us? She was bloody well following us! Why the fuck aren't you picking up your phone, Alexandre?"

I called Sophie back, my eyes on Pearl. I couldn't believe what I'd heard but I knew my sister; she would have done her homework. Sophie never made mistakes. Wow, Pearl had me fooled. First of all, she looked not a day older than thirty, with that tight, smooth body that even a twenty-five year old would have been proud of. I'd been dumb. I was so wrapped up in the romance of our relationship, I hadn't bothered to find out who she really was, what she did for a living. Damn it, I probably could have known everything within ten minutes, just by Googling her.

Pearl was gazing back at me, her face ashen. She knew something was wrong. My eyes had turned as cold as two sharpened flints—I could feel it myself. I never had been good at hiding my anger.

I looked at her. *Pearl Robinson, you've fucking betrayed me. I trusted you.*

Sophie picked up on the first ring and continued her rant without even saying hello. "Fucking Americans! They always have an ulterior motive. Always out to get something from you. Pearl Robinson is a fucking snake in the grass! I suppose you're shagging her as we speak!"

"No, I'm not, actually," I said coolly, my heart feeling as if it had been ripped out of my chest. Talk about a good performance. Pearl had me conned. Really fooled. There I was imagining that she had desperately fallen for me. I was the one who had fallen. Fallen hard.

Fallen on my goddamn face.

Sophie went on, "I hadn't put two and two together because it was her boss, Natalie something-or-other who'd sent me all those emails, begging us for an interview, to take part in their fucking spy-film. What have you told her, Alexandre?"

"Nothing," I lied.

"Because if you've spilt the beans about our business, it will be all over the papers, soon enough, or edited into some bloody documentary for the whole world to see!"

"Don't worry about it," I said, my heart pounding. Fuck! Pearl knew so much about my past. About Sophie stabbing my father in the groin. Me, trying to kill him off with rat poison…a fascinating story it would make: the CEOs of HookedUp both belonging in a loony bin.

"Does she know about the gems? Does she know about our highly illegal Mumbai deal?" Sophie screamed at me.

"Of course not."

"Get the fuck away from that scheming, lying bitch and never, ever see her again."

"Sure," I answered sadly, my eyes still fixed on Pearl's beautiful face. My insides were churning like a cement mixer. "Bye, Sophie, I'll call you later."

I pressed 'end' and let out a disappointed sigh. I shook my head, "Oh Pearl, oh Pearl." I was wondering how I'd be able to bear it—how I'd be able to stand not having her in my arms, not be able to fuck her, make love to her, see her face when she came, hear her moan with desire.

Her big blue yes widened with guilty innocence. Damn, she was a good actress. "What?" she asked.

"Why didn't you tell me? Why didn't you tell me who you were?" I was waiting for her to admit what she did, to offer me a reasonable explanation, but she just dug her grave deeper.

"What do you mean?" she said, her finger touching her nose. *Such a giveaway.*

That was her fucking response—that's the best she could come up with.

My lips pressed tightly together, my body tensed. I'd given her a chance to wriggle out of her deceit, but she'd blown it. I hissed between gritted teeth, "Is this what all this means to you? Having breakfast with me, spending time, making love? All this so you can go back to your fucking editing suite and plot out the next scene? The scene where Alexandre Chevalier and Sophie Dumas's pasts are revealed? Was *that* what it meant to you when we were in bed together? A ploy to get intimate with me and make me spill the beans about my private life?"

"NO! I mean…I…let me explain, Alexandre—"

"Explain what? That you lied to me? Oh no, not lied, that would have been too obvious. You omitted information. Omitted to tell me what your game plan was. Why didn't you just come out with it?" I lower my voice, "Because if you wanted to fuck me as part-and-parcel of your deceitful little package deal, I would have done that for free. The only difference is I would have fucked you harder, cared a little less," and I leaned down and whispered in her ear, "I would have fucked your ass off, pounded into you ruthlessly like you fucking deserved, so you couldn't walk for several days afterwards."

The people in the hotel restaurant were staring at us now. Fascinated by our domestic scene. Pearl's eyes were brimming over with tears—mascara running down her cheek. But she still couldn't come up with a decent excuse. She did what every woman does when they are caught out—she pulled out the sympathy card. But I wasn't falling for it.

"Don't fucking cry on me now," I said coldly.

"Please Alexandre," she whimpered, dabbing her tears with a linen napkin. The sympathy card wasn't working, so she laid out her next card on the table: The Queen of Hearts. "I love you," she sobbed.

Her words pinched my heart but I took a big breath and muttered, "Good try, baby."

She babbled on incoherently about the coffee shop—how she'd missed our talk, something about not giving a toss about HookedUp but wanting to focus on important things, like exposing arms dealers.

More important stuff. My point exactly. Sophie and I were just pawns to her.

I stood up, heat flushing through me, not wanting to listen to her bullshit, lame excuses anymore. She'd proven to me that she was your typical, ambitious, ball-busting career woman. Tough. Ruthless. Trampling over others at any cost to get what she wanted. I slapped a couple of hundred dollar bills on the table to more than cover the check. "Keep the change," I snapped. "Oh yeah, you left your gifts at my place—the pearl necklace, the kingfisher feather. I'll have them delivered to you—a little keepsake, a souvenir," I said bitterly, "so you can remember our time together." I turned on my heel and strode out of the room, not looking behind.

Pride before a fall.

10

That fall came a good week or so later.

Meanwhile, I had Laura on my case, not to mention Indira.

"Darling," Laura purred into the phone, "please let me know about France. I want to book my holiday but I also want you to *be* there. Like I told you, James won't be coming this year. I miss you. A lot. Call me."

Next voicemail: Indira. "Alexandre, please forgive me. I was behaving like a banshee. I don't know what got over me. Of course you're seeing other women, it's natural. We live thousands of miles apart from each other. I can completely understand. You were such a gentleman the other day, not wanting to take advantage of me. Please don't hate me because I flipped out. Water under the bridge? Anyway, I'm coming to New York to promote my next film and I'd love it if we could have dinner or something. Call me."

Next message: just tears and sniffling down the line. It must have been Elodie because I didn't recognize the number. She'd changed it so many times in the last six months, I couldn't keep count. Was there someone she was trying to avoid? I called the number back. No answer. I was tempted to set up a GPS tracking system on her phone. Something I didn't feel good about—I hated spyware of any kind, but Elodie was eighteen years old, new in New York with limited English, and so stunning that people stared at her when she walked by, despite her sneer, her black Goth make-up and her fuck-me-fuck-you-or-I'll-stab-you-in-the-eye-heels.

Women. They really were a handful.

I called Elodie back.

"Where are you, sweetheart?" I asked. I was sitting at my desk in my apartment, looking at a framed photo of Rex. I made a mental note of going to Paris to get him ASAP.

Elodie spluttered as if a drink had gone down the wrong way. "How did you know it was me?"

"Only about ten people have my number and I figured that if a number comes up I don't recognize, it has to be you. Are you okay?"

"I'm fine. By the way, do you still have that bodyguard who works for you sometimes?"

"Of course," I said, my jaw ticking at her out-of-the-blue, very worrying question.

"Can I borrow him for a while?"

"Elodie, what's up? Is someone following you?"

There was a long pause. I could hear street noises, her clicking heels. Then she answered, "No. No, of course not. I'd just feel safer, you know. I don't know this city so well."

"I'll put him back on the payroll full-time, then," I told her. "What about the new apartment? Will you be scared without a man in the house?" I had just bought her a two-bedroom apartment in Greenwich Village. She was going to get a roommate to share it with her: an old friend from Paris. "Maybe you should carry on staying at my place?" I suggested.

"No, it's fine. I love my new flat. Can't wait to move in. Listen I've got to go. Speak later." She ended the call and I sat there wondering what was going on. I got up and started pacing the room. I'd try and find out without compromising her privacy too much, but if my niece felt she needed a bodyguard, I sure as hell wanted to find out why.

The week dragged on. I tried to concentrate on work but everywhere I looked I saw signs of Pearl. I hadn't returned her gifts, mostly because I couldn't bear to let go of her memory. I didn't wash the shirts I'd worn because I could still smell her on the fabric. She was everywhere—even on my bloody iPad—in one of my goddamn lists.

Being a nerd, I write lists, something I have always done to make sure I'm on top of any situation. As I said, multi-tasking has never been my strong point by nature, so all thoughts, all ideas get written down. So being as busy as I was, with so many fingers in pies (and other places), I had to be on the ball.

I read the bullet points I had written about Pearl:

Problems to be solved concerning Pearl: needs to reach orgasm during penetrative sex. (My big challenge).
Needs confidence boosted—age complex due to American youth worship culture.
Need to get her pregnant ASAP due to clock factor—need to start family.

The list just went to show how hard I'd fallen for her and how much I had invested myself in her.

I expected her to call and apologize, the way Indira had. Pearl was in the wrong, and yet still, each day went by with no news. It was beginning to really irk me. How dare she fuck me over and then not even say she was sorry?

Then I started worrying about her, the way you do about members of your family. Was she alright? Had she died in some freak car accident? Then Sophie called and put my mind at rest. At least, for all of five minutes, until I started obsessing about Pearl again—pacing the room, wringing my fingers through my hair.

Sophie was in Paris. But even from long distance, I could feel her whiskers twitching, her claws sharpened.

"The gems are in Amsterdam," she started off by saying. "All good. They're with the best cutters, the best jewelers. We're going to make a mint. We'll need to buy some more real estate with the cash…distribute. I'd like to buy a brownstone on the Upper East Side, you know, for when I visit New York."

"Good idea, we should launder a bit."

"Launder. I hate that word—it's so crass. By the way, speaking of laundry, of your *dirty* laundry, we don't need to worry about Pearl Robinson anymore; she doesn't seem to be a threat. Looks like she's got bigger fish to fry."

"What do you mean?" I asked, ignoring her dirty laundry jibe.

"She's turned her attention to that Russian billionaire, that arms dealer."

"What Russian arms dealer?"

"You know, the handsome one, that young thirty-year-old Adonis-Casanova guy who's always strutting about on red carpets with supermodels. What's-his-face, you know, Mikhail Prokovich."

A stab of jealousy pierced my gut. Pearl was turning her attention elsewhere? "That blond guy? He's an arms dealer? I thought he was in real estate. He's an *arms* dealer?" I repeated, incredulous.

"A clandestine one. I doubt Pearl knows whom she's dealing with. He's very black market. He mixes with war criminals, soldiers of fortune, crooked diplomats and small-time thugs who keep militaries and mercenaries loaded with arms. But he's powerful. Very powerful. Pearl was seen having dinner with him just last night. All smiles, apparently."

I hated him already. I felt my fists clench into tight knots. What was Pearl *doing*? She hated arms dealers, was talking about exposing them in her next documentary. And now she was *hanging out* with one?

"What else do you know?" I pressed my sister, blood bubbling in my veins, jealousy rippling through every muscle in my body. This guy was sickeningly good-looking. Even as a man I could tell you that. Dashing, one of those square-jawed types that look like they've walked straight out of a cartoon strip. Blondish hair, searing blue eyes. Sophie was right; he was a red carpet kind of guy—liked to be seen. Cocky. With beautiful women hanging on his arm, and probably hanging onto his every word, as well. Jets. A fleet of flashy cars, some of them enviably cool. Houses all over the world. Every woman's fantasy.

"Sophie, what else do you know?" I demanded again in a low growl.

"That Pearl's been out to dinner with him, that's all. Him and some important guy from the United Nations. She's not just some sweetie-pie, naive American chick with big blue eyes and luscious lips, you know, Alexandre. She's a smart little operator, a user. She knows people in high places. Knows what she's doing. Obviously loves mixing business with pleasure. Anyway, at least she's off our case now, onto the next fool who'll fall for her innocent little act. Oh wait, before I go, how's Elodie getting on?"

"I think you'd better ask her that yourself," I said, not wanting to betray Elodie's confidence in any way. But my mind was now focused on Pearl, not Elodie. Sophie's words rang cruel in my ear… *"Pearl likes mixing business with pleasure."*

The more I thought about it, the adrenaline surged through me. Fuck her! Flirting and smiling with that fuck, Mikhail Prokovich? She was *mine!* I could hear my breathing getting more unsteady by the second. I was feeling hot and very bloody bothered. I loosened my tie; I'd been in a meeting earlier that day and was wearing a suit.

The idea of her being anywhere near another man was making blood rush to my head. Especially one as powerful Mikhail Prokovich. I got up from my desk and counted to ten to calm myself. But then I did the reverse, I started counting *down* from ten, and by the time I hit zero, I was out the door and into the elevator. I had to fuck her.

Before the Russian got his clammy hands on her.

I just hoped it wasn't already too late.

By the time I reached Pearl's apartment, my heart rate had doubled. Tripled. She hadn't apologized. She'd been using me. Using me to further her career. And now she was onto the next guy (her next project) without even a blink of one of her big, baby-blue eyes! Her whole "I haven't had an orgasm forever" was bullshit, obviously. Her little ploy to draw sympathy, to get gullible men like me all worked up and horny. To bring out our macho side—be *the one* to make her come, be *the one* to fuck her properly. Clever girl. Clever, clever girl. She'd hooked me in. Now she was moving onto the next guy.

She deserved a fucking Oscar.

Perhaps she won't even be home. Maybe she's on that son-of-a-bitch arms dealer's yacht by now, her lips clamped around a straw sipping cocktails, or worse…her lips clamped around his….ugh! The thought made my brain burn. But my dick was propelling me to her. Just thinking about her was getting me hard. I couldn't bear the idea of that cocky-faced shit touching her ass—that sexy, curvy ass, or kissing her beautiful lips. Maybe I was jumping to conclusions, maybe I was being paranoid, but I didn't want to let the distance between us encourage some gatecrashing jerk to push his way into her life.

The doorman let me in, and as he was reaching for the land-line to call her to announce me, I dashed through the lobby to the service elevator, thought twice and legged it up the back stairs, instead. I couldn't risk Pearl instructing him not to let me up, or halting the elevator between floors. I'd bang on her kitchen door until she answered—goddamn it, I *had* to have her. *Had* to fuck her. Remind her how good we felt together. Remind her that she didn't want any other man bulldozing his way into her panties. The fact that I, myself, was acting like the biggest bulldozer of all, escaped my one-track mind.

By the time I reached her floor, I was sweating. My tailored suit didn't help my frantic climb. I banged on her back door outside her kitchen. I stood by the trash bins, my heart pumping as adrenaline surged through me like a lion hunting its prey.

Pearl answered the door. James Brown's *Sex Machine* was blaring. *Good. She probably hasn't even heard the phone which is still ringing—the doorman trying to announce me.* She stood there, and I swear to God, my dick flexed hard within seconds. I was like an untamed animal. All decorum lost, all manners out the window.

I heard myself actually panting. "That'll be the doorman on the phone telling you that a rapist is on his way up to fuck you," I blurted out, not even thinking how crass I sounded.

She looked fucking beautiful, all poised in her business outfit: white shirt and navy blue pencil skirt and high heels. She must have just gotten home from work. My eyes raked her up and down and I even rearranged my crotch—that obvious—I had a hard rod in my pants. She looked down at my groin and bit her bottom lip. *Right, that's it—she wants to get fucked, alright.* My foot was wedged in the doorway so she couldn't kick me out. I pushed the door open further.

"Aren't you going to invite me in," I said, moving forward. She didn't have much choice.

"I don't know." *Oh yes you do know, you cock-teaser.*

"I have to fuck you, Pearl," was my answer.

I pushed my way inside and pressed her against the wall. *Sex Machine* pumping away was making me even hornier. I start kissing her, my erection pressed hard up against her, my hand fisting her hair so she couldn't move and had no choice but to get devoured by me. My tongue was licking her mouth and she started moaning quietly. I could see her nipples harden even though it was hot. No bra. I had to have those tits in my mouth. I pushed her arms up and pulled her shirt over her head with ravenous intent. I nipped her hard buds between my teeth, one and then the other, my hand up her skirt, the other cupping her round ass. I slipped my finger inside her saturated folds and surprise, surprise, her body was begging me to do anything I wanted to it. And I intended to. You bloody bet.

"You want to get fucked, Pearl? The way you fucked me over? The way you fuck men over to further your career?"

"No," she moaned, her eyelids fluttering in carnal stupor.

"No, you don't want to get fucked? I think you do. So. Horny. And. Wet. So ready for me to fuck you senseless, aren't you?"

I rammed my fingers up her higher, and she gasped. Her skirt was in the way so I unzipped it and ripped it down her thighs. The little harlot was wearing scarlet panties that screamed out, *fuck-me*. How fitting. I unbuttoned my fly opening. My cock was throbbing to get inside her. I got down on my knees. I had to taste that hot pussy. Had to stick my tongue inside her. I took those moistened panties between my teeth and peeled them aside, my teeth gripping them with lustful ardor. I could smell her, smell her sweet, fruity odor. My tongue darted inside her wet cunt.

"You want to fuck, Pearl? Because you're so much better at fucking than you pretend. Fucking people over, especially."

I so nearly didn't bother with sheathing myself with a condom. My instinct—like one of those soldiers using rape as a war weapon—was to impregnate her. Make her mine, even if it was against her will, and feel every juicy cell in her pussy without any barrier between us, but I relented, reminded myself how fucked-up that was, and rolled the condom reluctantly on my raging-hard erection. I didn't even take off my jacket, let alone my pants.

I pushed her red panties to one side and rammed myself into her ruthlessly, fucking her against the wall. I was half expecting her to try and stop me, but she was groaning with pleasure, relishing being 'raped' by me.

God, she felt good. I realized that this was something I couldn't do without. I had to have Pearl Robinson on a regular basis even if she *was* using me. By now, I didn't even care.

"I love. Fucking. You." I was growling, pounding her so hard I could feel myself ripping her open. She'd never had so much of me inside her before. I was holding nothing back this time.

She was loving every second, though.

"You like to get used, Pearl, or you just like using!" I said in a deep, angry voice, my mouth all over hers.

"I wanted to get to know you, Alexandre. I want to get to know you. All of you....every...beautiful...inch of you," she said, flexing her hips at me. "All…oh God…oh wow…oh God…" She could hardly speak as I thrust into her over and over, slamming her against that kitchen wall. She was clawing me, her mouth on mine, greedy for my lust.

"Is this what you want to get to know?" And I grabbed her ass in both hands so I could bring her closer, fuck her harder. "So. Tight. This. Tight. Pussy. Clenching. My. Hard. Cock." I felt her contractions like a pair of skin-tight gloves pressuring my erection. The red panties were also grazing back and forth against it, adding to my arousal.

Her nails were digging into my back—she didn't want to let me go. "You're so huge. Oh my…so enormous! I love you, Alexandre. I love you…fucking me."

"You love me, Pearl Robinson? Is that what you're saying?" I asked with irony. I was going to come any second. That *love* word went straight to my dick, even if it was a bold-faced lie. I burst inside her, my giant orgasm ripping through my center, and hers, with abandon, breaking my golden rule—not caring that I was coming first. I was moaning like a child, not a grown man. I felt weakened by my desire for her. She had me hooked—her smell, her pussy, like an exotic fruit. Her taste. Everything was driving me wild and had me spellbound.

The pulse of my orgasm faded to a tingle and I pulled out, but seconds later, literally seconds, I felt myself flex again. I had a flashback of our Skype sex phone call the week before—when I was in the limo on my way to Mumbai Airport—and I got her to fuck the sofa. Pearl and her sweet pearlette pressed up against the arm of the couch as she rocked back and forth in her white, schoolgirl panties. I wanted more of that, and I was going to get more. You bet. But with me 'live,' this time, not just us on screen.

I grabbed a cushion off a kitchen chair and pressed it onto the corner of the table. "Fuck the table," I told her. I peeled her red panties down her thighs so I could see her moistness, hot between her legs, and pressed my erection against the soft flesh of her round butt. "Push that hot little pussy up against that cushion," I ordered.

She did as she was told. A wave of desire shot through my whole torso. "Press harder," I said, putting on a fresh condom in haste. "Massage your clit back and forth against that table."

She obeyed me. Telling her what to do gave me a thrill and I gloated, *Eat your heart out you Russian cocksucker; this girl's mine!* I pushed the tip of my cock against her entrance—I could see her glistening gate to Heaven with my eyes. Every time she moved back, her wet slit bumped up against the crown of my cock. I was letting her tease me as it dipped in an out of her a couple of centimeters on each movement. She was moaning on every thrust.

"Gotta love this pussy," I growled like the horny lion I was. "It's warm and wet and shiny pink—like a beautiful shell. No wonder the Spanish call it a *concha*. Little sexy *conchita.*"

Her ass was high in the air as she was bent over, her torso flat on the table. I cupped her ass with one hand and with the other, took my cock in my closed fist and teased her, up and down, up and down her butt crack, then sometimes plunging all the way into the wet warmth of her folds, then pulling almost all the way out. She was writhing before me, her arms steadying her torso, flat-out on the table.

"Please Alexandre. Oh God. This feels incredible. Oh God!"

Then I started thrusting. I reminded myself that, this time, I didn't have to go easy on her. I had to remember that she was a selfish, career-getting operator out to *use* me. So I drove into her hard again, to remind her that two could play at the using game.

"Little. Career-getting. Pussy. Using. Me. And. Getting. Off. On. It." On each word I thrust into her and held myself still for a second. Pulled most of the way out then thrust back inside her. But this was no punishment for her, I soon realized. No, she started coming, moaning like the little tigress she was, her tight velvet glove contracting around me, which tipped me over the edge. I could feel myself thicken and I slowed way down, letting my climax surge through me in a blissful, throbbing rush. I moved languidly inside her, both of us coming simultaneously, something we seemed to do with ease. I was like a switch with her. Her gratification aroused me instantly, so when she climaxed, I did, too. Hard.

I collapsed on top of her, my body blanketing her smooth back, her glorious ass. "Pearl, baby, what am I going to do? I just can't keep away from you. I have to keep fucking you. Over and over. I just have to, I can't stop."

The problem was, that however much I tried to stay furious with her, I couldn't. When I spun her around to face me, she had tears in her eyes. A look of love. A look that said, *We are meant to be together, you and I. Please don't hurt me.*

And I melted.

The Russian flashed through my mind again. I couldn't risk it. I knew his playboy reputation, his bulldozer mentality. I had to get Pearl out of New York City for a few days. Just in case he came sniffing about.

Make her irrevocably mine.

If any other man even thought of coming near her, I'd fucking flatten him.

11

I took Pearl to my house in Provence. The ultimate test. Does it travel well?

It did travel well, *very well indeed.*

In fact, she traveled so well that we both joined, for the first time ever, the Mile High Club. We hitchhiked a ride on a French government jet—they owed me a few favors and I thought I'd cash in on one. No point contributing to global warming by taking a private jet ourselves—cadging a lift seemed like a good option.

Sex on a plane (there should be a cocktail named after that) was better than I had ever imagined. Of course, most mere mortals have to suffice with doing it in the toilet. Not us. We did it in full view, so to speak. Now Pearl and I were fully-fledged members. Not only that, but I found myself coming inside her without using a condom, without even consulting her first. What was that all about? A stake to claim? My dick acting as if it had a brain of its own, again? A mixture of the two, I guessed. I felt such relief to have her back in my arms after that week of lonely torture without her, that claiming her as mine in every way I possibly could, felt natural. The beast in me. The instinct to mark her as my property took over. Making her pregnant was the surest way, I supposed. Although, I truly *was* acting on instinct. The logical side of my brain was AWOL.

Did I forgive Pearl for not having come clean with me when we first met? Yes, I did. We spoke about it briefly on this flight. She told me that before she met me, she had imagined that I was a computer-nerd-geek. So when she bumped into me in the coffee shop, she was taken off guard—surprised by her beating heart and the powerful physical attraction we shared within the first few seconds of setting eyes on one another. She didn't want to blow it (that sounds like a bad joke, doesn't it?) She didn't want to jeopardize a possible romantic liaison because of a work project (which Sophie and I never would have agreed to anyway—and I think Haslit Films had cottoned on our reluctance by that point). So Pearl kept quiet about who she was. I understood. She presented herself, not as Pearl Robinson-documentary-producer, but as Pearl Robinson-look-into-my-eyes-and-tell-me-what-you-see. And what I saw was a woman needing attention. Lots of attention.

Besides, I wasn't the type of person to milk a grudge with a woman. I realized that during the week I hadn't seen her, I'd been climbing the walls.

Yes, I was falling in love with Pearl Robinson, despite her faults. Maybe even *for* her faults.

Although it was obvious that Pearl was in control when it

came to her career, she certainly wasn't when it came to her heart. I had captured her heart and that thrilled me. It was instantaneous for both of us. Cupid was in a good mood that day in the coffee shop and decided to zap us with his arrow. I had her tongue-tied, confused, disarmed.

It was evident that neither of us could keep away from each other.

Love is not logical. If it were, we would all be able to follow the rules and live in a nice, neat, square box. Love is a hurricane or a tsunami. It hits you when you least expect it. And what you have to work out…is how to survive it.

With Pearl, I had a premonition that I was up for a roller coaster ride with her, but I also had a very strong feeling, even then, that if I tried to get off, I'd fall flat on my face.

I knew that when Pearl woke up the following day in our bedroom in Provence (note how I say *our* bedroom—yes, it was getting that serious), she would be enchanted. The lavender fields were in full bloom, the scent of jasmine was also wafting through the French doors that looked out onto the stunning view below.

Who wouldn't fall in love with an old stone farmhouse in the middle of the French countryside? In the olden days in the South of France, people built their own houses stone by stone, getting friends and family to help them. A far cry from the multi-million dollar properties they have become nowadays. When I restored my house, I wanted to pay attention to each stone, bring out the beauty and detail of the workmanship—the sheer labor of what they had achieved by hand (no machines), all that time ago. I left it exactly the way it was originally; crooked walls, wobbly oak beams, wonky floors. I kept all of its charm, just added a swimming pool. Not a Hollywood-style pool—no bright blue or anything. I wanted it to look as if it had always been there and blend in with the landscape, organically.

I woke up early that morning as I had house business to attend to—I wanted to ensure that the elderly couple (who look after it when I'm away) had everything under control, and that the garden was in order. I wanted to let Pearl rise and shine on her own— soak up her new surroundings. I'd instructed Madame Menager to take her up some breakfast, while I took care of a few business and personal phone calls.

Last but not least, Laura, my ex. As I stood by the pool, white butterflies darting by me, the gentle sound of water tinkling from the fountain, I called her on my cell.

As I expected, she was not too thrilled.

"Laura," I began, "how are things?"

She had ears like a bat. "Is that your fountain I hear by the pool? Are you in Provence?"

"Yes, I am," I replied evenly.

"Alex, you promised!"

"No, actually, I didn't."

"I said you should wait for me! How long are you there for? I'll get on a flight today."

"Laura. No." I walked slowly from the pool area into the house and sat down on the sofa in the living room, where coffee, fresh-baked *brioche* and croissants awaited me. I spread some homemade jam I'd concocted myself (from my very own cherry trees) onto a croissant and took a large bite. I was half listening to Laura and her protestations and wondering what Pearl's reaction would be when she woke up here, in this beautiful, peaceful haven.

Laura droned on, "What do you mean, *no?* I told you I was planning a visit, I told you—"

I cut her short. "I've met someone, Laura, and I wanted to tell you directly."

Why I even felt I owed Laura an explanation, I have no idea. But I did. I suppose it was the whole wheelchair thing, the guilt I felt about her having suffered for so long. As silence rang in the air, my eyes strayed to the bookshelves where several of Laura's hardback books still lined the shelves. I needed to return them to her. Now that I had met Pearl, it didn't seem right to have my ex's belongings in my house. There was something else in those shelves I needed to deal with, too. Something Top Secret, hidden inside a multi-volume encyclopedia. I had cut out the middle and buried the incriminating evidence inside. Now that we had Wikipedia online, nobody used encyclopedias anymore—the stuff was safe, I decided.

Laura's silence still echoed down the line. I knew that the words, *I've met someone* would be a blow to her, even though she was married.

"Who is she?" she finally asked.

"I'll tell you when we're really serious." *Damn, that came out wrong.*

I didn't feel inclined to tell Laura Pearl's name because I didn't want her sniffing about my personal affairs. But at the same time, I wanted to nip any fantasy Laura might have had about rekindling our relationship…in the bud. Inferring that my relationship with Pearl wasn't yet serious was a mistake. It gave Laura false hope.

"Well, I'm sure you're having great fun but it won't last." She tittered knowingly. "Is she a local French girl from the village?"

"No, she's American." *Shit, why couldn't I keep my mouth shut?*

Laura's lighthearted tone changed several octaves. "So you brought her over specially? Imported her from *America?*"

"Listen, Laura, I have to dash. Take care. Send my best to James. You're both welcome to come for your vacation in a couple of weeks, when I'm not here. Bye."

Pearl and I spent the day by the pool, wandering about my lavender fields, lingering over a long lunch and drinking too much chilled rosé wine, pale as rainwater; the grapes from my own vineyard. I took her to visit my local villages, or rather, she took me. I let her drive my electric blue, 1964 Porsche Coupé, sunroof open, as we soaked up the sun and Nina Simone singing a song that reflected our moods, *Feeling Good*, as we sped by open lavender fields, and rolling hills of wheat and sunflowers—the summer landscape dotted with farmhouses and hilltop villages.

I can't remember the order of things that day, or exactly where and when each conversation took place, but we discussed a few important issues; namely the pregnancy topic. Knowing that Pearl was forty put our relationship on a sort of fast-forward. At least in my mind—there wasn't time to dither about. I'm a practical man. I'm also impatient for outcomes. I'd met Pearl, I couldn't bear to be without her, and she was forty. We didn't have the luxury of waiting around to find out if we were a hundred percent perfect for each other—we simply had to get on with it.

She didn't know that I knew she was forty. I was brought up to never ask a woman her age or discuss it with her. I was told it was bad manners. Pearl, however, berated me for having come inside her when we had sex on the plane. I guess she felt her freedom of choice had been tampered with. I didn't blame her. Talk about bad manners! The bulldozer had momentarily taken me over—I couldn't help it. But the upshot of it was (I know…*upshot*…does sound crude) that she admitted she did want a family.

There was another topic I'd been meaning to talk to her about: the Russian.

While she managed the steering wheel of my Porsche, I steered the conversation in another direction. "So," I began, "how are things in the documentary department, now that Haslit Films has given up on my company?"

Pearl's eyes were on the road. "Fine. Great. Natalie and I want to do a special about child trafficking in the sex trade. What's going on is really despicable. You'd think it would be getting better with so much publicity and so many arrests, but it's worse than ever."

"I really admire what you do, Pearl. Didn't you mention something about arms dealers the other day?"

"I sure did. That's another thing Natalie and I are focusing on."

"Oh yeah? Any leads?"

"My contact at the UN is pulling a few strings for me."

I turned to look at her. To gauge her expression. "What kind of strings?"

Pearl swerved a little too fast around a hairpin bend. I pressed my foot on an imaginary brake and sucked in a breath.

"Oh, you know, just organizing a few contacts," she said, with a nonchalant wave of her hand. *Keep your hand on the steering wheel!*

Was it my imagination or was she being cagey? "Anyone in particular?" I asked, trying to keep my voice casual.

"Oh, you know, just *contacts.* I prefer not to jinx things. Not discuss them till I have the goods in the bag."

The goods in the bag?? What bloody goods? "Have you met any of these arms dealers, personally?" I pried.

She just shrugged her shoulders. By this point, I could feel my pulse pick up; blood pumping hard. I felt aroused by jealousy, which in turn, made me feel possessive. Possessive, jealous, horny, irritated—all the sort of traits in myself I wanted to keep under control. I can't remember how I did it, but I veered the conversation toward Laura. I'd mentioned Laura earlier that day. I wanted to let Pearl know that there was an ex in the picture, be honest about it. Just in case Laura called and Pearl picked up the phone or something. But now I decided to toy with the situation; I just wanted to keep Pearl on her toes…let her feel that same stab of jealousy that was spiking my Latin veins.

"I'll show you some photos of Laura when we get home," I told Pearl, "and some letters she wrote me. When you see the pictures you'll understand why she left me for someone else." I knew what was going through Pearl's mind and she fell for the bait.

"Was Laura a *supermodel,* or something?"

"She was beautiful, both inside and out." *Outside, yes. Inside....A grand exaggeration on my part.* But I continued, blithely, "Yeah, she did do some modeling."

At least, I *thought* Pearl had fallen for the bait, but she coolly, not only changed gear, but changed the conversation back to the subject of my Porsche like she didn't give a fuck. Couldn't give a toss about my exes. Yet *I* was burning up. Why was she insisting on not mentioning that she'd had dinner with Mikhail Prokovich? My pride wouldn't let me delve any further, so I dropped the subject. But my curiosity had been whetted and the possessive gene in my DNA got the better of me.

What was I to do with a cool, independent woman like Pearl Robinson? She was forty. She had her own money, an amazing career, owned her own apartment; men no doubt, were desperate to date her and falling at her feet. She didn't *need* a man like me. Was my sister right? Was I just a sort of *Toy Boy* to her? Was she taking me seriously or just enjoying great sex? Women often confuse great sex with love. Maybe Pearl would wake up and smell the coffee. Find out about my fucked-up past and screwed-up head, not to mention my nutty family.

Not only did I want Pearl to think me the hottest thing since the sauna, but also the coolest thing since Mount Everest.

I was balancing a difficult act.

That night, one of my fears materialized. We went to a party nearby, given by my friend Ridley. Sophie appeared like a bat out of hell, wearing a black slinky dress, her hair loose and sleek. I had an ominous feeling she might show up.

Everybody's eyes were on Pearl in her sexy red dress. I mean, *everybody,* including my sister. As we walked in they were playing *Can't Take My Eyes off of You* by Franki Valli & The Four Seasons—the perfect song for Pearl. Charlize Theron was there, and people were getting them confused—that's how good Pearl looked. Some movie star was chatting her up, without any qualms at all—some blond guy, Ryan, who had been in a romantic, Kleenex type of tear-jerker movie—female film goers wailing with emotion at every scene. I knew this because of Elodie; she'd taken me to see it. That was before Elodie had become an Angry Young Woman. Now, it seemed, she eschewed the male sex in general, so I doubt even this Ryan character would have done it for her. And there he was now, brazenly hitting on *my* Pearl.

It was obvious to me that Pearl could get any man she chose. She didn't look a day over thirty. When I say thirty, I mean a beautiful, hot, sexy thirty. She looked amazing: tall and slim, but with killer curves in all the right places. Her skin and body glowed with health and fuckability. I know fuckability isn't even a word but it should have been coined just for Pearl because she oozed it from every pore. She was confident, self-assured, elegant. Despite her hot little dress.

Then *Wonderful Tonight* by Eric Clapton was playing and it couldn't have been a better song to describe how I felt about her.

But I knew I had to get her out of that party ASAP. Away from Ryan the megastar, and away from Sophie and her sharpened claws.

While Pearl was being flirted with, I located my sister, grabbed her by the wrist and pulled her into the kitchen, where I hoped we could be masked by a little privacy.

"What the fuck are you doing here, Sophie?" I demanded, with a smile on my face. *The HookedUp CEOs. My what a lovely sibling team they are! They get on so well.*

"Ridley invited me," she said in a singsong voice.

"Where are you staying?"

"At your place, of course."

"You can't just turn up to my house whenever you feel like it! Especially when I'm there with company."

"Company? I can't believe you're still fucking that cougar! In her slutty red dress, drawing so much attention. You *have* seen her, haven't you, Alexandre, doing the rounds, 'networking' as the Americans like to call it." She added in a whisper: "Four-tee. A cougar if ever there was one—I wonder what poor creature she'll hunt down tonight."

"Sophie, let me tell you something," I enunciated, pinning her against the fridge. "40 is just a number, forty is just a word. In five year's time *you* will be forty. In several year's time, every single young woman *out there* will be forty—that is, if she's lucky enough, and doesn't get run over by a bus, first. And most of these women, I guarantee you, will not look as hot as Pearl *ever* during their whole lifetime, let alone when they're forty. Stop pigeonholing people, especially Pearl. She's my girlfriend and that's final. Do. You. Understand?" I glared at her, my eyes burning through her and the smirk on her face. I had never felt this protective about a girlfriend before.

"Ooh, the Toy Boy's getting touchy! Have I hit a nerve?" She threw her head back and cackled.

No, but Pearl has. Pearl has hit a nerve. Every single nerve in my body.

I answered, "Sophie, I haven't felt this wide awake for years." It was true; every emotion of mine had been stirred. Anger, jealousy, fury, passion, desire, sympathy, compassion… Pearl had done that to me. Pearl had woken me right up.

"It's just a faze, Alexandre; you're just in lust with her, that's all. Mark my words… Oh look, there's Ridley; I must go and say hello. Please, dear brother, could you kindly unleash my wrist?"

"With pleasure," I said. And I got the hell out of her way.

I exited the kitchen and went on the prowl for Pearl. The party was in full gear. Glamorous people glittered everywhere. Champagne was flowing. A wild boar was being roasted on a spit in the garden; the aroma wafting through the open doors. Everybody seemed delighted, chatting in French or English, even Frenglish, clinking glasses and blowing air kisses. Everyone, except me, that was.

I located Pearl through a sea of floating gowns and penguin suits, marched over to her and pulled her away from the blue-eyed movie star. I nodded at him in a gallant, *This is my woman, move aside,* type of way.

I took her gently by her hand. "Pearl, we have to leave."

She shrugged her smooth, golden shoulder. My eyes scanned down to her peachy ass, accentuated by her red silk dress. *I'd have that ass, later.*

Meanwhile, I was hatching a plan in my head. We couldn't go home because of Sophie. We'd drive to a hotel. In fact, I'd take her somewhere really special—the French Riviera, the Côte d'Azur. To a stunning place on the southern tip of the Cap d'Antibes: the Hotel du Cap-Eden-Roc.

And I'd fuck her senseless.

12

My plan to fuck Pearl out of her mind backfired. By mistake, I got her drunk. We enjoyed too many vintage wines with dinner, and by the time we were finished, I had to carry her to bed. The wine, I think, was Pearl's way of blotting out the unpleasantness of last night: as we were leaving Ridley's party, Sophie appeared at the doorway, vampire fangs out. Pearl hadn't even recognized her but knew something was up when my sister practically spat at her: "Cougar!"

I felt so ashamed. Embarrassed. I suppose I hadn't understood the extent of Sophie's possessiveness toward me. She had attacked Laura in the same way, but when Laura and I split up, Sophie suddenly decided that the sun shone out of Laura's ass. Very convenient. But I hadn't felt the same sense of fury with Sophie concerning Laura that I was now feeling with Pearl. Pearl was bringing out my protective side.

I needed to deal with my sister, fast. Before she really fucked up my love life for good.

The wine, plus the long drive, made Pearl woozy. The hotel prepared us a candlelit dinner under the stars. Crickets were singing, and the Mediterranean waves lapped soporifically, inducing an intoxicating scent of sea and fresh air that had Pearl in a trance. She leaned back in her chair, sipping her Châteauneuf-du-Pape.

"Am I in Heaven?" she asked drowsily.

"I'm afraid so," I said with a guilty smile. "I've got you a bit tipsy."

"I'm tipsy on the aroma of wild thyme and lavender and France, not to mention this wine which is out of this world."

"I'm glad you appreciate it. A good Châteauneuf-du-Pape is like a beautiful work of art that takes you by surprise. It's not for everybody. It's earthy and sometimes fierce, the proverbial 'brooding' wine."

"Like you, you're a brooder," she said, pointing her finger at me, almost toppling over in her chair.

She has my number. "Why do you think I'm broody, Ms. Robinson?"

"Oh, Mr. Broody, Mr. Moody…you think I haven't worked you out? There's more to you, Monsieur Chevalier, than meets the eye."

"Honestly Pearl, I'm very basic. Boringly so." I tipped her a wry smile.

"Yeah, right, Michael Corleone with your illegal empire." She closed her eyes and inhaled the saline breeze as if it were her last breath. *My illegal empire? Did she know about the gems? And what lengths I would go to, to protect my loved ones? Michael Corleone, huh?…I always did respect that man.*

When Pearl opened her eyes again—her pupils dark like pools of fathomless ultramarine—she gazed at me questioningly, and asked, "Why, Alexandre, don't you just throw in the towel with HookedUp? You have more money than you need for several lifetimes. You said you wanted to get back to being creative, not just making deals."

My throat felt suddenly dry. Perhaps if Pearl hadn't been so tipsy, I wouldn't have admitted my failings so readily. "The problem, Pearl, is that making money has become addictive—the more I make, the more I feel I need. Power does corrupt, no doubt. I've created a kingdom, and like any king…." I trailed off. Pearl was rocking in her chair, about to pass out. I took her hands to steady her and thought about what I'd just said. I, like Pearl now, could topple. I was afraid to lose my crown. Sophie was part of my kingdom—the queen to my king, as it were. We were equal partners in HookedUp, so it would have been tricky to extricate myself. Her obsession with making money, and more money, and more, had rubbed off on me. But our relationship wasn't healthy—we were too entwined with each other mentally, as well as being business associates. A 'marriage' made in hell.

I was beginning to want out completely.

I got up from my chair and walked over to my beautiful Pearl. Her red dress reflected against the glass of deep wine, like blood, glinting under the moonlight. I took the glass from her hand and set it on the table—she'd had enough to drink for one night. "And you, Pearl? Do you care about money?" I asked, scooping her up in my arms and turning in the direction of our suite.

Her head flopped back and she grinned. "If I did, I'd be doing a different job, don't you think? Being a producer of controversial documentaries isn't going to bring me millionzz," she slurred. "I love what I do. I've had a lot of headhunters knock at my door offering me almost double but, you know, I'm not motivated by money." She nuzzled her head into my neck and kissed me there. I took in the sweet smell of her hair, of her sun-kissed skin, and carried her, like a baby, to bed.

It was true what Pearl said. I could tell that she really didn't give a toss that I was so wealthy. So if she didn't care, why did *I?* I *could* wind down HookedUp. Sell my share to Sophie—go back to being more creative. Sophie was meddling with my life, and without realizing it, destroying my happiness. I'd lay my cards on the table, I decided. Tomorrow.

So the next day, while poor Pearl was suffering from a morning-after-the-night-before hangover from consuming champagne, plus two different vintage wines (each paired with a different course of the meal), I started by explaining to her a little about my past. I told her that Sophie had once been a sex worker, that she was fearful of being poor again, and that she was like a mother to me after we left home when I was seven. I didn't get into the nitty-gritty details about her being a Dominatrix, nor about her eventually running the show and being a *Madame* with her own highly illegal 'house,' hiring other women to work for her. Too much information at once could have scared Pearl off. I tried to explain to Pearl Sophie's motivations but I think it came out wrong. It sounded as if I was defending my sister, putting her before all else.

Putting her before Pearl.

The look on Pearl's face after I'd admitted that Sophie was a sex worker made me snap, "Don't be judgmental, Pearl. Have you any idea how tough it was for Sophie? She was only seventeen when we left home. She was doing her best."

"I guess life has never gotten that….*tough* for me," Pearl replied, choosing her words carefully in an undertone which said, *I would never do something like that—never stoop so low.*

"*You* should understand, Pearl. Your brother, John, got involved with drugs and alcohol—it was his demise. People don't always do the right thing for themselves or others but it's right for them in that particular moment. You can never judge someone else's life or their choices—the path they take, because there are always two sides to every story. Or more. Sometimes there are multiple sides to someone's story."

"I guess you're right," Pearl answered, her eyes welling up.

I hadn't meant to bring her down by mentioning John's death, but I wanted to put us on the same par. I held her hand and we sat there silently for a while, both of us what-if-ing about our individual histories.

I thought of my mother, what she'd done, and my own shady past and wondered if Pearl would stick with me if she knew my whole story. Probably not. She was a wholesome, star-spangled, American girl who, after the initial novelty of great sex wore off, might decide she didn't want some screwed up Frenchman in her life. Was that why I had come inside her—to get her pregnant? So she couldn't get away from me, even if she tried? So that we'd always have a bond even if she left me?

We went for a swim in the sea and I watched Pearl in awe. She dipped and dived, her toes pointed like a dancer, and when she swam, she sliced the water like a sharp blade. Watching her do the crawl made my chest fill with pride, knowing that she was my girlfriend, knowing that this interesting, sexy, independent American woman had chosen me as her mate.

Still, there were undulations of bad feeling about Sophie, rippling between us. I sensed that Pearl had reservations; that there would be only so much she could take. I needed her close to me. Needed to be buried inside her. So after the swim, I took her to our suite. The more hooked on sex she was, I reasoned, the more likely it would be that she would never leave me, despite my crazy family history, despite Sophie's uncontrollable jealousy. Despite my dark side. I'd fuck her senseless. Literally. Make it so she couldn't see straight. Couldn't think straight.

Outside our suite, the cicadas were singing their summer song, thick in the pine trees. From our open balcony, the blue sea glittered beyond, and an aroma of pine and oleander, sweet as cake, wafted into the room, blowing perfume in the air. But the view that caught my attention was Pearl, herself. We Europeans are used to seeing topless women on the beach. So when Pearl took off her bikini and revealed two vanilla breasts, begging to be sucked they looked so tasty, I was instantly hard—instantly aroused by the forbidden, American fruit.

I gazed at my beautiful Pearl lying on the sumptuous bed, as she teased me—trailing ice cubes about those full tits; making the nipples pucker up into stiff buds that I wanted to stroke with my rock-hard cock. Yes, I wanted to fuck those tits.

"You're asking for it again, Pearl Robinson," I said.

She lay there seductively, her lips curved into a knowing smile, her smooth legs splayed open. She slid the ice cube down her stomach, then up and down her slick cleft, slowly inserting it inside herself. She gasped. My dick flexed, as it prepared itself to fuck her, throbbing with desire. I took off my swim-shorts—there was no more room and they were getting uncomfortable. I could feel how big I was—huge. I sauntered up to her, my cock proud against my abdomen, and straddled her on the bed, pinning her beneath me. She had hunger in her eyes; a look of lust that matched mine. I took a sip of champagne, and fed her with the liquid, letting it trickle into her luscious mouth.

I studied her oval face. Her blue eyes shone the same color as the Mediterranean Sea, with glints of turquoise, and faint freckles had appeared about her nose and cheeks. It gave her the air of a teenager. I still couldn't believe that she was forty—she looked so young, so fresh. And, as I appeared several years older than I was, we were an ideal match. We must have looked exactly the same age to anyone seeing us walk about, arm in arm.

The perfect couple in love.

"You're so beautiful, Pearl. So, so exquisitely *beautiful.* Your eyes…"

"*My* eyes? What about yours? They're green, but not really green, at all. They're like tiger's eyes with flecks of gold in them. *You're* the beautiful one, Alexandre. You take my breath away—every time I wake up with you next to me, every time you catch my eye, and when you touch me?"—she whispered in my ear and licked my lobe. I shivered, electricity coursing through my body, making my dick swell even more—"I can hardly—" she continued, with another swipe of her tongue—"function. And when you fuck me?"

Her attention switched from my earlobe to the rest of me. First, my mouth, which she kissed with fervor, exciting me so much that I couldn't take the ache in my groin anymore. I edged my way up the bed and slipped my throbbing erection between her lips. It was as if I were entering the twilight zone. Having her pouting mouth suck on me was the most erotic thing in the world. She flickered her tongue, moaning as she licked off my pre-cum, and I pushed my hips forward, rocking slightly, languidly, fucking her mouth. Damn, it felt good. I could smell her sweet taste of sex as it lingered in the air with the scent of pine and sea. I needed to lick her all over; explore every crevice, every secret place. So I did.

I started under her arms, then I swirled my tongue about her breasts and aroused nipples. I listened to her groan as I trailed my tongue over her salty, tanned body, down her pretty stomach and then between her legs, fluttering my tongue on her clit, but taking it away again so I knew she'd be begging for more. I sucked her toes, licked her delicate ankles, up her calves, behind her knees and along her thighs…up, up, up to her core, pale against her tan because, like her tits, that part of her had been hidden from the sun. She was writhing on the bed, wet and wanton, her pussy glistening like the little pearl it was. I circled my tongue around her engorged nub and tasted her nectar.

"Please Alexandre. Please fuck me." She bucked her hips into my mouth as I sucked and teased her, and she murmured something about a dream she'd had the night before, featuring a big, black stallion.

"You want to ride me, baby? Is that what you want? Ride me like a stallion?"

Now that I'd made Pearl come in several different ways, it was time for something a little more experimental. I could have carried on and had her come in my mouth, but she wanted to ride? Sure, why not. Let her ride my cock. The *Reversed Cowboy, hmm…nice.* I put myself beneath her, and maneuvered her so that she slipped her wet warmth onto my pounding erection, her head facing my feet, so my view was of her glorious, round ass.

"Show me what you've got, cowgirl. You call the shots with your pussy pistol." I grinned. I had her exactly where I wanted her, and it felt great. My hands were either side of her little waist as I guided her up and down. Up and down. She was stroking my ankles at the same time—so sensual. Mixed with the image of her behind, I was a happy man, indeed.

"Love that peaches and cream ass, Pearl. Love that. Tight. Wet. Pearlette."

I still hadn't worked out if Pearl was full of it, or not, about her orgasm (or lack of) history. Sometimes, I felt suspicious.

a) because she was bloody good in bed and…

b) because she seemed to come every single time with me.

Every time, except when I practically raped her and fucked her so hard against her kitchen wall—but even then, I got her on Round 2. Here she was again, going crazy for me. Moaning while she fucked me, her hands cupping my balls (where did she learn that?), easing me out of her, and then slapping the tip of my cock about her clit. Driving me fucking crazy. Teasing me. Nobody had ever turned me on so much as Pearl.

"That's right baby," I breathed, "lasso my cock with your tight, tight pussy, you cowgirl."

My hands played with her nipples, rolling them between my fingers as Pearl continued her horny ride, rocking back and forth. I grabbed her ass, and feeling myself about to come, started my *one, one thousand* count. Luckily, I didn't have to keep it up for long, because when I tilted my hips forward, she started moaning. Tiny beads of sweat broke out on the small of her back, and her contractions told me that I could break free and let myself go—hard. Fuck, I was coming like the bloody Niagara Falls; my cum bursting inside her, as she slammed down on me, swallowing me deep.

"Oh Pearl, oh Pearl, you beautiful thing," I murmured as she sank all the way down, grinding herself into me.

"I'm coming Alexandre." *Yeah, babe, I know.* "Oh God, oh…."

She started twiddling her clit with her hand and it brought on another rush from me. And her.

"Fuck, Alexandre, I'm coming again. This has never happened to me. Ever! I thought it was impossible to come twice in a row."

A crooked smile played on my lips. "*Mission Impossible*," I said, and started humming the tune, as my hands roamed around Pearl's small waist and then over the curves of her ass. Was she lying?

Or was I a fucking *god* in bed?

Whatever, I was on fire. I had to keep fucking this woman. I felt like an animal and needed more. Had to get her pregnant. Had to have more, more, more! More of my seed inside her. More of everything. Pearl was my life tonic. My elixir.

Once her orgasm had calmed, I pushed her off me and spun her around so she was on all fours.

"Hold onto the headboard, baby. I have to keep fucking you." I grasped her ass with my hands as I slid into her—she held on, her head leaning against the soft headboard as I consumed her. Not in her ass, no, but entering her from behind. Her. Sweet. Hot. Addictive. Pussy.

She was groaning. I knew I was being unreasonable. Dominating. Bestial. But I couldn't stop.

"Love. Fucking. You. Fucking. This. Sweet....Jesus, Pearl, what is it about you? All I want to do is make you come, come inside you." I kept pumping her. Fucking her relentlessly. I knew she must have been sore as hell but I had to admit, I liked that idea. I wanted her to feel me. Raw. Untamed. A man who at times, would lose control. A man that had to have her. Own her. Take all of her. All *mine.*

But I slowed down. A voice inside my head told me I was acting like a dick. I pulled out slowly and went to 'kiss it better.' Kiss that sweet pearlette that I'd been treating like a hot, juicy cunt. Pearl was too special for me to be losing control like this. I flickered the tip of my tongue around her bruised center and she whimpered with pleasure...but I could taste myself, taste her, taste sex and it got me ravenous again.

The beast was back. I had to come inside her, once more. I entered her again.

She cried out, "Oh God Alexandre, I love this!"

"This ass is...oh fuck...this creamy, peachy, hot ass has got me hooked...your hot, sweet pussy..." Pearl had me beside myself. I cupped both butt cheeks with my hands and carried on with my assault as I drove myself into her. In. And. Out. In. And. Out. She was tight like a glove around me. The sensation was incredible. "This ass belongs to me. *All of it* belongs to me," I heard myself growling. I eased up and stilled myself, knowing I'd gone too far. Knowing I'd pushed poor Pearl to her limits, my Neanderthal instincts had taken me over.

But what do you know? My rock-hard, throbbing cock, still inside her, had her contracting all over it. She started moaning, her nipples as hard as cherry pips, her golden hair flopped like bands of silk over her shoulders.

She moaned, "Oh God…Alexandre, I'm coming again. This is insane. What are you doing to me?"

I flooded into her. I was coming again, too. Every sweet sensation was in my cock. As if every brain molecule was there. It was ruling me. Ruling her. This was my true queen: Pearl Robinson. I wanted her to reign with me; run my empire by my side.

"Je t'aime, Pearl. Je t'aime," I whispered, my climax surging through me like flashes of white lightening.

She didn't reply.

I just told her I loved her. That was a huge thing for me. But she said nothing.

I wished I knew what she was thinking.

Wished I knew what was going through her mind.

13

I guess I should have known that when things seem too good to be true, they usually are.

Sophie really outdid herself this time. She had made me so furious that I began to have fantasies of having her shipped off to a desert island and dumped there, with no means of communication. I'd have care packages flown in by parachute but she'd have to survive on her own. Because boy, was she being one hell of a Megabitch.

I was happily basking in the sun on the hotel rocks by the sea, having sex flashbacks of Pearl, when I discovered Pearl had done a runner on me. While I was busy being Master of the Universe; taking care of business calls and making more money that I didn't need, Pearl had taken herself to Nice airport, alone, and never wanted anything to do with me again. I listened for the forth time to her phone message on my voicemail (the message had come in when I was otherwise engaged). It was too late to catch up with her. More fool me.

"Alexandre—what can I say? I've left. Obviously. I received a message on my cell from Sophie who seemed to know every intimate detail of my sex life. I'm glad your 'challenge' worked out for you. And for me, too. It was a real eye-opener—an experience of a lifetime. It was beautiful. Beautiful because I believed in it. But now I've found out that it was just a game for you. I know that it could never be the same between us again. You said it yourself: the biggest sex organ is your brain. And my brain is shot to pieces right now. Goodbye, Alexandre. Good luck with Rex—shame that cute dog and I will never meet. Bon voyage."

Never meet? What the fuck had happened?

I called my sister.

"Alright, what have you done this time?" I demanded when she picked up.

"You'll get your share of the rubies and stuff, don't be impatient, Alexandre."

"I'm not talking about the fucking rubies, I'm talking about a rare pearl—more important than any gem. Pearl. What did you say to her?"

"Nothing she doesn't already know."

"You told her stuff about our sex life, didn't you? Stuff I have never, ever discussed with you. Why did you spin her a load of lies, Sophie?" I shouted, my voice on fire.

"Not lies. The truth. She's a stalker. A cougar-stalker almost twice your age. I found things on your iPad, too. You should lock it with a password, you know."

"My iPad is private, for fuck's sake. I had no idea you'd be gatecrashing my house. Plus, I write stuff down in English so people like *you* can't snoop. More fool me, obviously."

"Google Translate is my new best friend, Alexandre. Sorry, but I couldn't resist taking a peek."

My stupid list about Pearl, I remembered. *That's what freaked Pearl out and made it look as if I'd betrayed her confidence.*

I said coldly, "You and I are over, Sophie. From now on, speak to my attorney because I can't deal with you anymore. I'll find a solution to HookedUp. Meanwhile, stay out of my fucking life."

"She's too old for you, Alexandre. What's more, she was trying to stalk you. I was just looking out for you."

"You, yourself, know that Pearl doesn't look her age, Sophie. And Pearl and I have moved forward. She was not *stalking* us, per se. The past is the past and I want that woman *in my life.* As I said, stay out of my affairs. You and I are DONE."

Sophie was silent. I could hear her hitched breaths on the line. "Shit, you're really in love with Pearl Robinson, aren't you?" she said in a shaky voice.

"Yes, I am and I'm choosing her over you, Sophie. So either get with the fucking program, apologize to Pearl, be nice to her for *evermore,* or get the fuck OUT of my life for good, because not only are you making Pearl miserable, you are making *me* miserable, too."

"Okay," she muttered in a quiet voice.

"You mean it?"

"Yes, I do. I'm sorry Alexandre, I didn't know she meant *that* much to you. I don't want my little brother to be unhappy, I really don't. I care for you too much."

"The damage may be too great. She might not even take me back. She's a nice girl, Sophie. A nice, wholesome girl who doesn't need a couple of dysfunctional French nutcases in her life. I'm hanging up now. You'd *so* better make it up to her in the future. That is, if she and I even *have* a future. She might not want me now."

I clicked end and dialed Pearl's number. I suspected her cell would be off, but still, I just wanted to hear her voice. I left three messages in a row, explaining things and I prayed to God, Jesus, even (my *Personal Jesus)*, that I could make things right again, and that Pearl hadn't given up on me for good.

I flew by helicopter to Paris. I *had* planned to do this with Pearl, of course, so she could meet my mother and we could collect Rex and take him back to New York with us. That part of the plan still stood; I needed my dog with me now more than ever, not just for myself and for Rex, but as bait to catch Pearl. Even if she hated me by now, and loathed Sophie's guts, surely she wouldn't be able to resist my loving black Lab? I refused to give up.

I *would* win Pearl back, no matter what.

When I saw my mother, I took a double take. People say that the woman you end up choosing will resemble your mom, and I laughed to myself. I *could* see Pearl in her. Tall, elegant, poised. Beautifully dressed. Blonde hair and large blue eyes—her complexion flawless. What lay beneath her cool exterior, though, nobody would have guessed. I had still kept her dark, dark secret;

hadn't told a soul, not even Sophie.

Maman was reading a book in the living room, a romance, no doubt—she was hooked on them. She loved the dominant alpha male, the type that rode up on horseback and swept a lady off her feet and galloped off with her into the sunset, the lady protesting but secretly delighted that the hero wouldn't take no for an answer. I slipped in quietly and observed her lying back on the sofa, shoes off, her feet up, and I wished that her real hero, my father, hadn't turned out to be such a demon. Wished that she could have been stronger, more resilient, because what happened in the end—the finale—could have been a scene right out of a horror story. She was smiling as she read, and as I stepped closer, I realized that it wasn't a book she was holding in her hands, but an e-reader.

"You're very modern, I didn't think e-readers had caught on yet in France," I remarked.

She jumped up and hid the thing behind her back. She looked mortified, her cheeks flushing a deep pink. "Alexandre. Darling! How wonderful to see you."

I came up to her and kissed her on both cheeks. "Did I interrupt something, Maman?"

She quickly switched off the contraption and composed herself. "No, of course not. Just a non-fiction, non-descript book, you know. Quite dull, actually."

Yeah, right.

She smoothed her hands over her skirt. "Where's your friend? The girl you said you were bringing to meet us?"

"She had an important meeting in New York, sadly. Had to get back early."

"Oh. How disappointing. This is the first time you've asked a woman to come here to meet us so I was all excited. I figured it must be someone very special to you. I've got all sorts of delicious treats for dinner."

"Yes. Yeah, she is special to me. Look, Maman, I'm so sorry but I can't stay long. I *also* need to get back to New York. I just came by to say hi and pick up Rex. I'm sorry you went to so much trouble for dinner, I feel terrible. But we have a jet waiting for us; I'll need to get going any minute."

"A jet? A *private* jet?"

"Yes, I didn't want Rex to travel in the hold."

"I know you're doing very well, Alexandre, but a private jet for an *animal?"*

"Sure, why not? Speak of the little devil!" Rex came bounding in from his walk with my stepfather who stood in the doorway awkwardly holding his leash. Ever since I had started making so much money, my stepfather felt redundant. *As if a man's merit is measured by his wallet.* But I guess that's how he felt. I stroked Rex's soft black ears and kissed him on the nose. "Thanks for looking after him so well."

Silence was thick in the air, save the tick-tock of a grandfather clock in the hallway. The house was replete with antiques and Persian rugs which gave the atmosphere an even more somber air. More reminders, I supposed, that I had furnished this house with these luxuries. You can't buy love. Only fear, respect, and resentment. My stepfather smiled at me uneasily and came over to shake my hand, and patted me on the back.

"Still in flip-flops and jeans even when you can afford the best shoes and suits that money can buy," he quipped, eyeing my feet disdainfully. It was only a matter of time before he suggested I get a haircut.

He was a tidy, attractive man but he lacked charm and charisma, something my father had oozing from every pore. That was when he wasn't carrying his dark passenger about with him—the character who took him over at any unexpected second. If only my stepfather knew my mother's secret. *If only he knew.* He'd probably pick up the phone and call the police, I suspected. No wonder she stashed her erotic romance behind her back when I walked through the door. He would have been shocked. He saw her as perfect. The man had no idea whom he was married to. Not *a damn clue.*

Still, he wasn't beating her up, so in my mind, he was worth his weight in platinum.

"Look, I feel so rude to do this to you, but the jet, even though it's private still gets a slot, you know, a take off time. Rex and I really need to get going. Come and visit me in New York. Any time. There are some great Broadway shows, fabulous restaurants—"

My stepfather cut me short with a chuckle. "We have the best food in the world in Paris, why would we be tempted by foreign cuisine?"

"Whatever," I answered. "But you know what? You'd be surprised what you discover when you scratch beneath the surface. When you dig deep, you never know what you may find."

My mother gave me a look that was more potent than a poison dart. "Bye darling, she said. "You'll need to *leave* now so you don't miss your private jet. Bye, Rex, baby," she said, cupping Rex's head and giving him a kiss—and she added with dry sarcasm, "Do send us a postcard from New York, sweet doggie, and let us know how you're getting on with the American cuisine."

I winked at her and smiled. My stepfather eyed up my mother—her seamless perfection—my comments flew right over his head.

Good. I wanted it to stay that way.

On the flight back to New York, I nodded off. Perhaps it was the hum of the plane—whatever, something reminded me…

I'm entangled in this web of ferocious filth. Fifteen years old and seeing stuff that no person could ever imagine in the span of a whole lifetime. I'm a cog in this wheel of destruction that I brought upon myself. Round and round—there's no end. The woman is pleading with me, "If the president says no to the peace deal and the French leave, the Rebels will kill us all. The French can't leave. We owe you our lives."

She's on her knees now, trembling, her hands clutching the material of my combat pants.

I look down at her, a specter of a woman, her hair matted with dirt, dried blood on her makeshift dress, as mosquitoes buzz around us in the hazy, dusty heat. She has been witness to horror. Her uncle was chopped up into tiny pieces in front of her, her younger sister decapitated, but she's grateful to be alive after ten rebels raped her consecutively at gunpoint. I hold her hand. What else can I do? What can I tell her? I can't assure her that everything will be okay, because it won't. These little villages are swollen with pain, each on the frontline of terror and war. A country broken and maimed.

No matter how many rebels I kill, they double in droves. Like angry, maddened wasps. Fearless. Relentless. Some of them even younger than I am. Just children. Children! Young boys wielding machetes and rifles almost half their bodyweight. It's them or me. It's kill or be killed.

But still, some of these 'Rebels' are children.

"I'm sorry," I say to the woman. Behind her I see the smoke and ashes of what was her house, burned to the ground. Yet she is still grateful. Grateful to be alive.

A man who must be in his late twenties, his eyes hollow graves, tells me, "My youngest cries herself to sleep every night. They took my wife from us, dragged her into the street and shot her. Like a wild animal, they shot her in the head. My daughter sees images of blood before she goes to bed at night. Please help us. You have to stop the Rebels. Please don't abandon us."

I jerked up in my seat, sweat dripping on my back and brow. The memories had snuck up, unexpected. The shadows of war. The horror that had been buried in some dark corridor of my mind had been unleashed once more, letting in the demons which were keen to knock at my brain's back door.

The words tumbled out of my mouth as I rolled them on my tongue, "The Ivory Coast," I mumbled to myself. It sounded so romantic—just the name conjured up a tableau of elephants, yawning sandy beaches, and thick forests. But for me it was one long nightmare, not the glamorous dream I had conjured up. Joining the French Foreign Legion had been a wild impulse. I lied about my age. I was just a lad of fifteen bursting to explore the world. An idealist. How are boys meant to know that fantasies will crumble to dust right before their very eyes?

I got up, ambled rockily to the airplane toilet and splashed my face and the back of my neck with cold water, trying to shake the cruel pictures from my mind, imbedded there like crimson etchings. I replaced the graphics of blood and gore with fields of lavender, the undulating waves of the Mediterranean—anything to let a sliver of peace ease its way into my assaulted brain. I splashed more water into my eyes, on my chest, my stomach, in the hope that it would help wash away the ghosts intent on sneaking into my soul. Because when you've been in war, your soul is seeped in black, however hard you may pretend it isn't. It's your secret. A secret you don't share with your loved ones because the pain, the dark knowledge of the truth, would be too great for them to bear. You have to convince yourself you did the right thing. You can even believe it. But your soul will never lie to you.

The adoration shimmering in Rex's eyes was tonic to my battered psyche. Dogs are great forgivers. Dogs don't care who you are, what you've done, if you haven't had a shower (the stinkier the better, right?), or how much money you have. As long as they get fed and watered, walked and loved, they'll stick by you. Rex was traveling in style but he was oblivious. He was about to live in one of New York's swankiest districts with a private roof terrace which boasted a lawn and trees and a view to Central Park. I had even hired a dog walker-nanny for him, Sally, who'd need to stay over sometimes if I was away on business. I didn't want Rex to be alone. Spoiled much? You bet.

Rex…my buddy. The one who could forgive all. Because as far as he was concerned, there was nothing to forgive in the first place.

He was excited by his new home, rushing and sniffing about,

exploring the three floors of my apartment as if there was buried treasure somewhere. The staff had even bought him treats and toys. I guess they knew their way into my heart was through my dog.

Everything was almost perfect. I was setting myself up with the ideal family situation. Beautiful home, people to help me run it, money galore, dog….but the most important ingredient of all was missing: Pearl.

She hadn't responded to a single one of my messages. Text, voice messages, emails. Zilch. She had obviously had enough. I'd have to work really hard to win her back. But I was confident I had a good chance. *Feelings like that don't count for nothing.* With all the women I'd been with, it *felt* to me as if Pearl was genuinely in love with me, more than any of them. But who knew? She hadn't said the words, even though I had laid my heart out to her.

It was nine a.m., New York time. I was sitting by my desk at home, listening to *Miss You* by The Rolling Stones, trying to do something other than obsess about Pearl. She'd be at work by now, I imagined. Rex and I had arrived at my apartment at 3 a.m. I didn't feel tired, so we walked around Central Park. I practiced some Taekwondo moves—I needed to keep my black-belt polished, so to speak.

I still like to do that sort of thing—toy with dangerous situations, walk about in dodgy places at night under the cover of darkness. Places where muggers and drug addicts could be hanging out. Keep myself alert. Sharp. When you've been in war zones the way I have, you've got eyes in the back of your head. Forever. The fear, like an author's sharpened pencil on a page poised to write, needing to write, never abandons you. You don't want it to because it's what you trust, what you rely on, even though it once nearly broke you. Fear is your friend. I'm a man who obviously needs adrenaline. Rock climbing. Surfing. Sex. Taekwondo. Hanging out in Central Park at 4 a.m. These things keep me alive. Keep me sharp as that pencil.

Besides, I had a Pit-Bull cross by my side; Rex's secret. He could pin a person down at a moment's notice if I gave the signal. His gentle Labrador side had people fooled.

I must have checked my cell twenty times. Nothing. Pearl. Pearl. Pearl. Her name rang in my head so many times, that by the end of the morning, the word 'pearl' sounded surreal, as if *my* Pearl was disconnected somehow, as if our relationship had been just a dream.

I wondered what direction I should take to win her back. Then again, she deserved better—*maybe I should just leave her in peace.* My mind was in turmoil, vacillating between the two extremes. I wanted her back. But if I pursued her, I didn't want to just show up at her work or apartment. I'd played that card.

I was going crazy. Lack of sleep…the memories swirling about my brain…my dark past telling me to let her go—to allow her get on with her life without me. But my burning heart and the hole in my gut couldn't bear to even entertain that thought. I needed to convince her to stay with me; not run away anymore. I didn't want to hound her but I did want, at the very least, to know how she was doing. I'd need to talk to her and explain, but right at that moment, I knew she was sick of the sight of me. Sick of Sophie. Pearl would need time to simmer down. I needed to keep the bulldozer at bay.

At least for a while.

First, I needed to sort out the tangled web of madness that Sophie had spun us into. No, I wouldn't turn up at Pearl's work. I'd write her a letter and have it hand-delivered to her apartment, with the pearl necklace that she'd left behind.

I found the choker in my bedroom, tore off my T-shirt which I wrapped around it. Only afterwards did I realize that the T-shirt was two days old and must have stunk of my sweat, but I didn't have time to do everything with decorum. Rex watched my every move, following me around my apartment, as if to make sure I did the right thing. I strode into my office, grabbed a piece of paper from my desk and hastily wrote a note:

Darling, precious Pearl,

You are my pearl, you are my treasure. Don't deny me this. Don't deny me the love I have for you.

When you left my heart broke in two. The Spanish describe their soul-mate as 'media naranja'--the other half of the same orange. And that is what you are to me, the other half of me, the perfect half that matches me. I have never felt this way before about anybody. Ever.

You think I betrayed your trust. No, I would never do that. Sophie snooped at my iPad and saw my personal notes. They were written in English so I never imagined she would bother to translate them. Call me a jerk, call me a nerd for making notes concerning you. But here they are. (I have copied and pasted this). This is what she saw:

I printed out the nerd-notes I had on my iPad (how shameful, how embarrassing!) and attached it to the hand-written part. It was the only solution. *Better for her to think me a geek who wrote everything down than a liar:*

Problems to be solved concerning Pearl:
Needs to reach orgasm during penetrative sex. (My big challenge).
Needs confidence boosted – age complex due to American youth worship culture.
Need to get her pregnant ASAP due to clock factor. (Want to start a family with her.)

I scribbled on:

I feel embarrassed showing this to you but it is the only way I know how to explain myself. I write lists and notes – I write them for everything – you know that.
When I first set eyes on you in that coffee shop, I was smitten, instantly. I remarked to Sophie how beautiful you were. Sophie commented on how easy American girls are, how they jump into bed with anybody at the drop of a hat. I told her, that in your case, I thought I stood very little chance – that you looked sophisticated and classy. (Given that I had never been with an American woman, I had no idea if what she said was true). It was disrespectful of me to discuss this in French with her while you were standing right there before us when we were all wait-

ing in line. I apologize. But that was then.

This is now.

Now I have found my Pearl I do not want to let her go.

I will fight for you. I want you in my life.

I have made a decision. I am giving over HookedUp to Sophie. I will still keep shares but will no longer be involved in the daily decisions of running it. I'd like to start up a new enterprise – a film production company and I will be looking for someone to run it (production skills mandatory). I wondered if you would consider yourself for the job?

Here is the necklace. It belongs to you, and only you.

A squadron of kisses,

Your Alexandre

P.S Rex has arrived and wants to meet you.

P.P.S For the present time my family members will no longer be staying at my apartment when they visit New York.

I decided I'd deliver this to Pearl's apartment myself. I called Sophie. I knew she'd still be having her 'power nap', six hours ahead, Paris time, but I didn't care; she owed me one.

She picked up but didn't even speak, just shuffled about, breathing into the receiver.

"It's me," I said curtly.

"What is it? Is Elodie okay?" she asked in a weary voice.

"Fine. Just fine. Listen. I know you did all that super-sleuthing about Pearl so I'm assuming you know everything there is to know about her."

Sophie groaned. "I told you I'd get off her case and I will, Alexandre. I've even been thinking of ways to make it up to her. Just to keep you happy."

"I appreciate that. Sophie, I need her best friend Daisy's phone number or contact address. The redheaded British girl who lives in New York. Do you have it?"

"Somewhere, I guess," she replied in a bored drawl.

"I need it now."

"Can't you find it yourself?" she said with a long noisy yawn.

"Yes, I *could* but I thought you were trying to make things right, Sophie."

"Okay, okay, I'll call you right back, I'll need to locate it."

I went into the kitchen, opened the fridge, which suddenly struck me as being absurdly large, especially for a bachelor, as I now hopelessly was. Would I be living alone forever with this massive thing, stuffed with enough food to feed several families? With no family of my own to feed? It didn't matter how much money I had. It didn't—as Hélène pointed out—matter how big my dick was, if I didn't have the right person to share it with, to create a family with.

I brought out a bowl from the fridge and Rex wagged his tail, expecting a treat. Would it be just Rex and me, then, if Pearl decided she's had enough? Two, tough, single males, roaming Central Park at night, daring anyone to fuck with us? I dug my hand into the bowl of blueberries and stuffed a handful into my mouth. Rex seemed to be interested in the blueberries, too, so I threw him a couple which he caught mid-air. My cell buzzed. It was Sophie, with Daisy's home phone and cellphone numbers. Even her address. Christ, my sister was such a stalker. I was glad to have her on my side and not as my archenemy.

I called Daisy, my heart inexplicably racing.

"Hello?" she said guardedly.

"I'm sorry to disturb you, to call so early—"

"Look, please, I'm not interested in buying your product, please don't call this number any—"

"It's Alexandre Chevalier," I interrupted.

"Oh." There was a weighty silence and then, "How on earth did you get this number, is Pearl okay? I just had breakfast with her, I—"

"You just had breakfast with her?" I said with hope.

"Excuse me, Alexandre, I'm not sure why you're calling me."

"Can we meet up?" I asked, and then instantly regretted my question. She must have thought I was hitting on her. Great. That's all I bloody needed.

"No, we can't meet up. I'm busy. If you want to see Pearl, she'll be at work by now. Call her."

"Look Daisy, that's why I'm calling *you*. I'm sorry to impose but I need to talk about Pearl. I just want to know if she's alright. She won't answer my calls, my emails, my texts."

"Good girl," I heard her whisper under her breath. Was she talking to her daughter or referring to Pearl?

"And I don't feel inclined to barge my way into her office when I know she's busy and too furious to see me right now," I added. Not only was that true but I wasn't feeling my greatest, with the surge of Foreign Legion memories battering me, bashing my self-worth to a pulp, my *raison d'être*. Right now, I felt Pearl deserved better than me, but still, I couldn't let her go.

"Look, Alexandre, I'm not Pearl's keeper. I can't help you. You really shouldn't be calling me in the first place."

"I know. I'm sorry, but I just want to know if she's okay. We had an argument. About my sister. I won't go into it but I assume Pearl—you two being best friends—has already told you everything."

There was a measured beat of silence and Daisy said languidly, "No, I don't think she even mentioned you, Alexandre. I mean, in *passing*, yes. Said she just got back from France but…you know, Pearl is a very busy, *in demand* woman. She doesn't have time for any nonsense."

I paced up and down the kitchen, blood roaring in my ears. Pearl hadn't even mentioned me to her *best friend?* Or only did so *in passing?* So…she really didn't give a fuck, after all. She would just get over me in a flash. *Shit!*

Daisy went on coolly, "Look, Alexandre, Pearl is the kind of woman who has men queuing up to date her. Literally. Men go crazy for her. Extremely wealthy. Important. Interesting. Men. It won't be long before someone snaps her up. I mean, men propose marriage to her all the time."

Marriage proposals? Yes, well that would make sense. She was forty. Wanted a family. She wasn't going to hang around and watch opportunities pass her by.

Daisy carried on, "She's beautiful. Clever. She's a catch. She's extremely busy with work, too. You know, she has a project about child traffickers, and another one concerning arms dealers—both in the pipeline. Important, life-changing stuff that the world needs to know about. She doesn't have *time* for silly games, or people who dick her around."

Those two words—*arms dealers*—sent a bolt of fury through my gut. That fuck Mikhail Prokovich would be moving in on Pearl any moment.

Daisy talked on, "If you want to catch a woman like Pearl Robinson, Alexandre, you'd better pull your socks up. I know it's summer and you probably aren't even wearing any socks—" she snickered at her joke.

She was right…I looked down at my flip-flops. My bare chest. Apart from taking off my T-shirt, I still hadn't changed out of last night's clothes. I had a five o'clock shadow, dog hair all over me, and apart from brushing my teeth that morning, I felt pretty grungy. I probably looked like a backpacker about to set off for a round-the-world trip. I imagined Pearl at her office; elegant, suited-up, heels. Legs smooth and golden. Cool and relaxed, talking on the phone to clients or in the editing room. A mover. A shaker. And me? I had lost the plot. So much so, I was calling her best friend for clues. This whole situation was ridiculous.

"I'm so sorry Daisy. I haven't slept all night. I don't know what got into me to call you. I just wanted some news of Pearl and didn't want to bombard her with my presence, you know. I've kind of been there, done that—don't want overkill, you know. I just wanted news of her, I guess. I couldn't bear the silence. Please don't tell her I called you, though."

"Alright, I won't. But think about it, Alexandre. Think about it carefully. Either fuck off and leave her alone, or do something big. You know what I'm saying? If you want Pearl you'd better step up to the *big* league and do something to really impress her. I mean, *really* impress her. We'll keep this conversation between ourselves. At least for the moment. I'm sure if you get your shit together I'll hear about it from her."

Tough cookie! "Thanks, Daisy," I said, making a mental note of never crossing this fiery redhead. "Good to get your take on it. See you around." I hung up.

I stuffed another handful of blueberries into my mouth, mulling everything over thoughtfully in my mind. Rex stared up at me, his head cocked to one side, as if to say, *Well, what are you waiting for?*

"You're right, Rex," I said, patting him on the head. "I'll impress Pearl, alright. This is it. *Make or break.*"

She had teased me, calling me Michael Corleone. I wouldn't let her down:

I'd make her an offer she couldn't refuse.

14

On my way over to Pearl's apartment to deliver the necklace, I decided to call Sophie. I knew she had an important meeting that she didn't want interrupted. Too bad. Even if busy, I knew she'd pick up her cell. Sophie was one of those people who was bitten by curiosity—couldn't bear to leave a question unanswered. So even a ringing phone was too much to pass up. And she never left her cell on voicemail in case she missed out on some elusive deal. She had a team working around the clock for her: investors, hedge fund managers, people on her payroll with their noses to the ground, sniffing like pigs for truffles. Not only that, but any country could be calling her at any hour, any second. A president. A mogul. A Russian oligarch. A billionaire Indian. Even The Queen of bloody England. Yes, believe it or not, there were people out there with even more money than us, and Sophie wanted a piece of each and every juicy pie.

Just as I had announced in my letter to Pearl, I decided that I was getting out of HookedUp. That I couldn't take the antics of my sister anymore. *I'll call her. Put her to the test.* I knew what the result would be, but I just wanted to hear the words come out of her mouth. I stopped by a deli and bought some fruit. I dialed my sister's number.

"Sophie, I need that big diamond," I demanded, when she picked up on the second ring.

"Oh it's you again," she groaned. Are you eating something?"

"An apple."

"I hate the way you can only get three or four kinds of apples these days. You know, there used to be over ten thousand varieties of apples in England, alone. Now all we have are—"

"I need the diamond now. Today," I told her with my mouth full.

She hissed into the receiver in a whisper, "Are you fucking nuts? a) the diamond's the most expensive stone out of the lot of them—we already have a buyer at seven million and b.) it's in Amsterdam with the jewelers—excuse me gentlemen, I just need two minutes to end this call—" I heard my sister's clipped footsteps and a door banging closed. She continued, "What the fuck are you doing interrupting this meeting? You know how long I've waited for this."

"I knew I shouldn't have let you do all the organizing of the gems yourself. Get that fucking diamond on a plane now! I need it for Pearl's engagement ring." I wanted to hear my sister's reaction just to test her, and I couldn't have been more spot-on.

She cackled with laughter like one of Shakespeare's Macbeth witches. "N-O," she spelled out. "No. You're *marrying* her? Oh my God, she's really got you by the balls this one, hasn't she?"

"That's all I wanted to hear. Confirmation of how impossible you are. How little you care when it comes to my wellbeing. I'm finished with HookedUp, Sophie. I'm going to start up a new venture. You can buy me out little by little—I won't squeeze you for all the money at once. Have fun in your meeting with that scheming son-of-a-bitch, Mikhail Prokovich."

"How the hell do you know he's part of this meeting?"

"Because I'm aware of how your mind works, Sophie, like billions of dollar bills wrapped about each brain cell. I've also heard from a source of mine that he's suddenly become interested in doing deals with HookedUp. Maybe he fancies you, who knows? But he seems to be all over everyone like a rash, right now." I bit an angry chunk out of my apple. "Doing business with that shifty bastard? No thanks. Another reason I'm out." I hung up.

I didn't want *that* diamond for Pearl. No. I had a better idea—something even more special. A one-off. A piece of history. Something that belonged to a princess. My museum contact who'd secured me the ancient silver stater (my 550BC coin from Greece that brought me luck), had told me about the most stunning diamond of all: something that was worth far more than seven million dollars.

That would be my engagement gift.

But first, I needed to make sure that I gained entry into Pearl's apartment. I couldn't do a re-run of last time when I dashed up the back stairs; the doorman would be onto that trick. Pearl still hadn't returned my calls or messages. The chances of her even letting me up when she was obviously still pissed at me, were slim. It seemed a lifetime ago that we'd been swimming in the sea in Cap d'Antibes, but less than twenty-four hours had passed. She was playing it cool. Maybe she'd stay that way. She might even feel inclined to send the necklace back, the box unopened. All my plans of asking for her hand, like some knight in shining armor on a quest, could be smashed if I didn't get to see her face to face.

I had to come up with something good.

Something really good.

Several hours later, I clanked my way up the fire escape of Pearl's building on the Upper East Side, carabiners jangling off my belt. Before climbing up, I had told the young doorman that someone had called 911 about smoke in the building, and he believed me.

I was clad in all the right firefighter gear but had abandoned the jacket somewhere further down below because it was still very hot from the late summer sun—I was sweating—beads of moisture trickling down my chest and abs. I felt bad for firefighters; they had to wear this stuff to work, yet not so bad that I didn't know the magic it spun. Women have always gone wild for them. I was hoping that Pearl would be no different. Perhaps, I thought, she'd just laugh at me—I looked like a cliché, Playgirl centerfold. At least I'd get her attention.

"Excuse me, ma'am, I said, peering through the kitchen window after I'd made my way up to the eleventh floor, "I heard there was a fire in this apartment." *True. The fire of Pearl's wrath.*

Pearl stared at me, her mouth dropped to the floor, but then her expression changed. She wasn't angry, nor did she laugh at me. A naughty smirk, yes, and a suppressed giggle at my outrageous outfit, but the second I laid eyes on her through the glass that separated us, I knew I was forgiven.

I pulled up the sash window and gatecrashed my way inside, surprised that the burglar alarm hadn't gone off by now; my big black boots stomping on the tile floor as she appraised my sweaty body, her melting blue eyes taking me in with approval.

"You nearly had me fooled but your accent gave you away," she said with a grin, no doubt brought on by the incongruity of the scenario: a faux French firefighter.

I wanted to ravage her she looked so beautiful: her golden arms hung cool by her side, her blonde hair loose about her shoulders, her scent of flowers and magic which always had me intoxicated. But I felt so much more than just pounding physical attraction for her. My heart was bursting through my sun-warmed chest: I was going to ask this woman to marry me. I yearned to start a family with her. All this, I was going to spell out to her.

When the moment was right.

I longed for her whole; her heart, her soul, her body, and every tiny emotion that came along with that trinity.

The good, the bad, the happy. And even the miserable. Because I knew there'd always be tough days up ahead. I'd be there for her. I wanted to wake up next to her every morning, smell her scent, hear her smooth voice. I'd even settle for a grumpy voice, as long as she was there beside me.

I was brimming over with love for Pearl Robinson. And I knew that if I carried on without her, I would only be half the man I was capable of being. Rich, powerful, successful; all those things men strive for in this world are nothing without the right mate—just sand in an egg timer that will come to an abrupt stop if you can't turn your life around.

We kissed, our mouths as one. I licked her all over, devouring her taste, her nectar, her essence, then carried her over my shoulder where I deposited her on her four-poster bed. I had to lie with her, make love to her—feel her every muscle, soak up her every cell. The firefighter garb seemed absurd by this point. It had helped me achieve my goal—to catch her attention. Get me into her apartment.

I jested with her, teased her with 'spanking' (an excuse to slap my cock against her glorious behind). I nipped her, pretending, with a sulky, downcast face, that she needed to be punished for running away from me, abandoning me. An old trick to re-balance the equilibrium of the relationship. I could feel myself falling and I needed to pick myself up.

"Get this garb off me," I said in a solemn voice. "I feel claustrophobic. I need to lie with you, Pearl. We've played enough silly games, it's time to get serious."

She was the student and I was the teacher—at least that is what I was striving for. Hoping to have some kind of command over her so she wouldn't run from me again. But in my soul, I knew that Pearl was her own person. She would never truly be mine. How can you own a free spirit like Pearl?

She put on some music which answered my question. *Je T'aime, Moi Non Plus*—I love you….Me Neither. *The 'me, neither'* said it all. Yes, she loved me, but I knew she wouldn't take any crap from me. I had a vision of her by the sea in France, looking over her smooth tanned shoulder, which she shrugged as if to say, *Catch me if you can*, and with a toss of her blonde mane, she dove into the water like a mermaid from the rock where she was perched.

Here I was, coming to catch her, but a presentiment, deep down inside told me, that in the end, Pearl would never be completely mine.

But I soldiered on, determined. I stroked her soft, golden hair and laid all my cards on the table, face up, "You're unique, Pearl, I've fallen in love with you." There—she had my vulnerability, my weakness laid out before her like a crudely woven carpet for her to walk all over if she wished, each thread visible, each weave part of my soul.

She smiled serenely and took in a long breath, but didn't answer me. She still hadn't told me she loved me yet. I did what came naturally when I felt insecure: my cock flexed at the softness of her velvet skin, her erotic scent, and I entered her, stretching into her wet, welcoming warmth. My power, my security: my big cock that had never let me down. It was the only tool I had that I knew how to use with precision. Everything else was new to me. I was ill equipped in the art of love. I hadn't known *true,* burgeoning love before—how it can burst your chest open and bring tears to your eyes. How it can sneak up on you and take hold of your gut and twist it into a pit of fear and loneliness when you think it has escaped you. Those twenty-four hours without Pearl had me as vacuous as a shooting star on impact—reduced to a particle of pale dust.

I controlled her sexually but in every other respect she held all the cards in her realm. She was the Queen of Hearts, the

Queen of Cups. All I could do was fill her in the way I knew how. I pushed myself into her until I felt her tightness cling to me, my security returning like a welcome friend.

I punctuated each word with a thrust, "Will. You. Marry. Me. Pearl. Robinson?"

As usual, she deflected the love question. I hadn't meant to ask for her hand in marriage this way. It was cheating. Using my sexual prowess to reach my goal. My insecurity had me thrusting harder inside her, grinding my hips slowly; making small figures of eight. The number eighty-eight. Infinity. A number that would keep going infinitum and would last forever, unbroken. I could feel myself expand as her walls gripped about my throbbing cock—she was on the brink. I sucked her hard nipples which I knew would push her over the edge, and then slammed my mouth on hers, my tongue ravishing her as I fucked her slowly, pulling out so my crown massaged her sweet clit, and then pushing back inside again, rolling back into the figure of eight, my hands like a vice about her smooth shoulders. She started screaming, writhing about beneath me. I had her, yet I *didn't* have her, and it was killing me.

So I asked her again, "Will you marry me, Pearl?"

She was coming hard, her orgasm so intense that I felt her unraveling beneath me, her fingers knotted in my hair, her tongue lashing on mine with so much carnal desire that she couldn't even speak—she just moaned. She bucked her hips at me, her skin misted with sweat, and hooked her legs about my calves as she dug her nails into my ass. Christ, she was like a tigress with her prey. Her climax was consuming her so intensely that her mind was blank.

I silently begged for an answer. I needed to know that she wanted me in other ways, too; spiritually, mentally. My cock was a fucking double-edged sword. But her folds, so snug around every stiff inch of me, clenching me like a fist, pushed me over the precipice. I let myself go, the rush of climax spurting hard inside her as her extended orgasm kept rippling through her beautiful body, uniting us in one detonating, fire-cracking explosion. She quivered and trembled under me as I groaned with deep, carnal satisfaction.

Only to be replaced with a flutter of insecurity, seconds later. *Say yes, God damn it, say the word,* I willed her silently.

"Oh yeah, oh yeah, baby," she whimpered, "this is….oh my God…oh…YES!"

That wasn't a 'yes' in my book! Then again, asking a woman to marry you while you're fucking her was hardly playing it by the rules. "What are you saying yes to, Pearl?" I breathed into her mouth as her orgasm wavered through her quiet moans, her body still writhing, her kisses still wet on my tongue.

But she still wouldn't reply coherently, only languid, brain-numbed moans escaped her lips.

I decided I'd ask her properly the following night. I'd just have time to buy the piece of jewelry that had been put aside for me: a vintage pendant that belonged to a white Russian princess. I'd have it adapted into a ring, especially for Pearl. Big bucks shout. If I paid the jeweler silly money, maybe he could have it done in time. I'd set up a dinner à deux at the top of the Empire State: king of all skyscrapers worldwide, at least in my opinion. I knew the owners and I was sure they'd do me that favor.

And if that didn't bloody well give me a bona fide 'Yes,' then

I'd be lost like a wayward ship on a stormy ocean about to go down.

I *had* to have Pearl.

For my own sanity.

15

Pearl was so busy at work that it took me three days to pin her down for our rendezvous. She was free for dinners but I needed to know that she could take a day off, too—I wanted her to be reeling, delirious, drunk on love for me.

I was nervous about popping the question—as my old friend Shakespeare so rightly put it: *There's many a slip twixt cup and lip.* Those three days crawled by, my heart jumpy, my solar plexus churning with anticipation.

Edgy as I was, it gave the jeweler time to do a beautiful job on the ring. It shimmered brightly, its myriad hues and unusual oval cut made it glitter, even in the dark, and it was so huge that it almost looked vulgar. *Eat your heart out Elizabeth Taylor*—this was a rock to be reckoned with.

Although they will tell you that it is 'impossible to accommodate requests to close down the Observatory at the Empire State for proposals,' when you pay the right person the right price, anything is possible. Pearl and I had the rooftop to ourselves.

It was perfect. The sirens and sounds of the city were muted by distance, the buildings, in a panoramic sweep below were almost like glittering pieces of Lego. The cars were just toys, smaller than my thumbnail, and the lights of Manhattan, Queens, Brooklyn, and New Jersey twinkled as far as the eye could see. The breeze was cool because we were so high up, but not chilly; the summer evening caressed our skin amidst a cloudless night, the stars blinking with swathes of the Milky Way dusted above the skyline like a pastel painting. The Empire State's saxophone player was there, playing haunting jazz tunes that set the mood.

Pearl was wearing a long, flowing gown in silk chiffon. Pale pink. I was wearing a Nehru jacket and suit that I'd had tailored in India. I kept dinner simple; I didn't want it to distract from the evening; champagne throughout—Dom Pérignon1953 with fresh strawberries and a selection of endless hors d'oeuvres (prepared by a French chef I'd hired), that kept arriving at our table—treats to nibble on while we gazed at each other, or walked about admiring the glorious view. Pearl looked exquisite. I hadn't seen her in a long gown before. I was glad that I was giving her a diamond that belonged to a princess because she looked every bit the part. We wandered about the observatory, peering down to the nuggets of light below, glittering, shimmering—the way Pearl glittered and shimmered.

A whoosh of breeze blew Pearl's thick blonde hair, making it billow behind her like swathes of gold, and in that moment I took her hand and got down on one knee. Her lips quivered into a knowing smile.

"My knight," she said. "The name Chevalier does you justice."

Still on one knee, I kissed her hand and said, "Pearl Robinson, will you do me the honor of being my damsel, of sharing the Chevalier name, of being my wife?"

Tears sprang to her eyes and she didn't answer. *Was she about to reject me?* I asked again, third time lucky, "Pearl, will you marry me?"

"I thought you'd forgotten, gone back on your word," she whispered, choking back tears.

I stood up and laid my arms about her shaking shoulders. *Note, she still hadn't bloody well answered my question!* "What do you mean?" I said bewildered.

"You asked me to marry you when we were making love and I said 'Yes,' and then you didn't mention it again. I thought you'd changed your mind."

I laughed. "Oh, Pearl, what am I going to do with you?" And then I put it to her once more, "Pearl Robinson, "Will you marry me, goddamn it?"

She squeezed me close and I smelled the sweetness of her hair, her breath. She leaned back and I kissed her in the hollow of her neck, on her lips, and on the tears that were flowing down her cheeks. "Of course I will, you fool," she told me with a little laugh, "I've wanted to marry you forever."

"I'm afraid I don't have a ring," I said. "Things are a little tight with HookedUp, right now. Do you mind waiting?"

She wrinkled her nose and gazed at me, love dancing in her blue eyes, "I'd be happy with a ring made of tin as long as the world knew that I belonged to you. And as for HookedUp going through a rough patch? I make enough money for us both to live on. We won't starve, don't worry."

You see, that's why I wanted to marry this girl. She didn't care about money. She was genuine and true. She did not show even a flicker of disappointment about not being given a ring.

I led her back to our table and poured us both some more champagne. I looked over to the saxophone player and gave him a quiet nod. He began to play *Manhattan Serenade,* and then the waiter brought out a tall, tiered cake, covered in fresh white lilies.

"Cake?" Pearl exclaimed. "And such a grand one? This beautiful evening has me speechless."

"It's not just any cake," I said with a wink. "Here, I'll cut you a slice."

"Really, I'm sure it's delicious but I don't think I can eat anything more," she said, patting her stomach. "Can we do a doggie bag?" she half joked.

"What? And let Rex get his chops all over this masterpiece? Just a small slice," I insisted, cutting a large chunk.

"Really, I couldn't, I'm so full…what on earth is that inside…it looks like…Alexandre, what the…?"

I pulled out a small red box from inside her slice of cake, licking the icing from my fingers and wiping the box with a napkin. "Open it," I said. "Go on, it won't bite."

Pearl gingerly took the box and bit her bottom lip in concentration, bracing herself—maybe for a ring made of tin. She looked at me, and then at the box again. She opened it and gasped. It was almost the sort of gasp she made when she came—blown away, as if in shock, as if that sort of thing could never happen to her.

"You like it?" I asked with a sideways grin. How could she

not? But then again, after what I'd said about HookedUp being in trouble, she might have imagined this ring was from a Cracker Jack box. It was so flashy, so ridiculously sparkly that it could have been fake.

"Alexandre Chevalier," she said. "Alexandre Chevalier…what am I going to do with you?"

"You're going to marry me," I said.

16

In the next couple of months that followed, I got to know a new facet of Pearl's nature: her stubbornness.

She was refusing virtually every offer of mine.

"Pearl," I said, as we strolled through Central Park with Rex, golden orange leaves falling before our feet, "please be reasonable. See sense. I don't want to do a bloody pre-nup." I took her by the hand and stood in front of her. She needed to look into my eyes. She wanted to sign this unromantic contract, stating that if we were to ever split up, she would take nothing that wasn't hers before the wedding.

She sighed and said, "Alexandre, I'm just being practical. You've worked so hard for your money."

"I've worked hard so I can share it with someone special, have a family, live a real life. I don't give a shit about the money itself."

"Ah, you say that, but what about your fancy classic cars,

your house in Provence that needs looking after, your apartment and Rex's nanny? That stuff doesn't come for free."

She was right. I'd gotten so used to having money I didn't even think about it. "*Our* apartment," I corrected her. I laced my fingers through her thick mane and drew her close to my face. "Anyway," I said with a brooding look in my eye. "I will. Not. Hear. Another. Fucking. Word. About. A. Pre-nup. Is that crystal clear?"

She threw her head back and laughed as Rex jumped up on me, concerned about the raucous I was making. "You see? You're upsetting Rex when you're so bossy!"

I walked along, silently brooding. Furious with her stubbornness. I'd have to fuck that out of her later, when we got home from work that evening. Make her acquiesce to my wishes. Worse than the pre-nup nonsense, was the wedding itself. She'd decided to wait until winter—had always, she told me, fantasized about a white wedding. But I knew the real reason. She was testing me. Using our engagement as a trial period to make sure she was doing the right thing. Fair enough, but it did little to ease my anguish….*Many a slip twixt cup and lip*. Why, I asked myself, couldn't we just get on with it? She was stalling and I didn't know the real reason behind her breezy, casual façade.

"White wedding," I mumbled, knowing, at least, that Sophie had made amends and was paying for a designer wedding gown that was going to cost her a cool seventy grand. "We could get married right here, today. Have a *golden* wedding—all these autumnal colors—wouldn't that be beautiful? In the boathouse, right here in the park? I could serenade you in one of those little boats like a Venetian gondola man and sing you that Italian aria.

And Rex could be our witness."

Pearl laughed again and nuzzled her head into the side of my neck. Hmm, she smelled so wonderful; the essence of woman, of sweet, sensual delight. The sort of smell that cannot be described however hard you try. She was sensual, all right, but as stubborn as a wild rose.

She stroked her hand over the bicep of my arm and nipped her bottom lip between her teeth. I could feel my cock flex. Yup, I'd really fuck her good and hard when we got home. I couldn't wait.

"You know, Alexandre," she said squeezing my arm, "you must be about the fittest male specimen I have ever laid eyes on." Then she slapped her hand on her mouth and cried, "No! How can I say that? There is someone, who, I have to admit *does* have a better body than you. Is even more toned than you. Maybe stronger. I know it's cruel to be honest…but…" She winced with a pitiful, sympathetic look on her face.

Slam! A wave of jealousy surged through me. I squinted my eyes at her and asked coolly, "Who?" I imagined my leg swinging into this character's chest and knocking him down flat in one, easy, Taekwondo kick—I'd show him who was stronger.

She burst out laughing again. "So easily roused with envy, aren't you?"

"Who is this buffed-up character?"

"Well," she began, "he's black."

"A black guy?"

"Black and very beautiful. Younger than you. Loves running. Very active. Friendly. Handsome. Adorable. Actually, it was love at first sight. The second I saw him I knew he was special. Stole my heart, really. Definite competition for you, Alexandre. I mean, I know I shouldn't be saying this to my own fiancé but it *is* the truth."

I finally twigged. I pinched her butt, teasingly. "So wicked, aren't you? So *femme fatale* to get me worked up about my own bloody dog! I knelt down and Rex came bounding up to me, skidding along the wet leaves, careening into me like a block of concrete. "Black and beautiful, friendly, adorable and very…" I slapped my hand against his rock-hard thigh muscles, "*very* compact."

Pearl knelt down, too. She was dressed for work, wearing a navy blue suit. She kissed me lightly on my nose and whispered, "I love to provoke you, love it when you get just that *little* bit jealous."

"What, me? Jealous? Don't be silly," I said. "I knew you we're kidding all along,"—I winked at her— "I'm far too self-assured to let envy get in my way. You'd better get yourself to work, chérie, or you'll be late. I'll walk you there."

We made our way behind the Metropolitan Museum where we could cut through the park to her new office building.

In an attempt, not only to cement Pearl's career and make her dream come true to work in feature films, but to also keep her under my wing, I'd bought out the company she worked for, Haslit Films, making it part of a new firm, HookedUp Enterprises. It was separate from HookedUp and had nothing to do with Sophie. I designed the deal so that Pearl and her ex boss, Natalie, could be equal partners.

But Pearl wouldn't accept HookedUp Enterprises as a gift. No. That stubbornness, again. Stubborn as the hook of a woman's bra on a first date. Pearl would only accept the position as director, working for a salary, refusing a share—just a percentage of future deals, instead. With me as silent partner. No special favors. She even insisted on having a contract drawn up with lawyers. She was the consummate professional—very irritating for me. I could have made her an extremely wealthy woman. But there was no way in this world I was going to convince her to take the profit and call the company her own.

She wanted to *earn* her riches, herself.

Another thing: she refused to sell her apartment. Just in case. *In case of what,* I wondered? She was renting it to someone on a one-year lease, while living with me, but *would not sell it. It was her nest egg*, she explained. I tried to convince her that she could have thousands of nest eggs. All the bloody eggs she could have dreamed of. Enough to make soufflés with. Omelets. But no. She wanted it *her* way. Financial independence from me, obviously. *Just in case.* She felt she had to prove herself.

I supposed it was from all those years of being self-sufficient. Two people had died on her: her brother, John, from an overdose, and her mother from cancer. Her surfer-dude dad had abandoned them when she was just a little girl, and Anthony, her other brother, was a self-centered jerk, or had proven himself to be, thus far.

Pearl was used to fending for herself, and however hard I tried to cajole her, to comfort her into believing that I could look after her, and *would* look after her, she was adamant that she could do it all on her own.

That should have been a warning siren but I just put it down to her pride and a reluctance to change the status quo.

I had told her that I felt more comfortable with 'a mature woman who had lived, who had suffered knocks and bruises,' but I was beginning to pay the price; Pearl didn't trust me a hundred percent, however much in love she was.

All in good time, I told myself as I gazed at her now beside me, her golden hair shimmering in the morning autumnal sun. I needed to be patient. She had a broken wing that had not completely healed.

At that point, I still didn't know what, or who, had broken that delicate wing.

"Jesus Christ, Pearl," I groaned as I dragged myself off her; loath to break up yet another incredible session of lovemaking. Fucking? Lovemaking? Both words described what we did best. Really, sex was designed for us. Us together, anyway. With Pearl it was always delicious. Intense. Physically the best I'd ever had. Yes, and that even included Hélène.

I was still hard. "I could go on doing this all day long," I said, planting a kiss on her lips and letting my eyes celebrate her lithe, curvaceous body, still slightly tanned from summer. She moaned sleepily and took in a long, satisfied breath, her orgasm still lingering.

But I had to catch a plane to London and I was already late, so I tore myself away from her side and went to have a shower. I'd hoped that Pearl would come with me to London, show her the sights, eat in my favorite restaurants. I wished that she could just generally hang out with me on business trips, but she was a career girl and she had her own plans, her own agenda. The fact that Hookedup Enterprises was a toddler learning to walk made Pearl relentlessly busy.

Her brother Anthony was coming to stay for a few nights so I was happy, in that respect, to leave them to their family reunion.

When I sauntered back into the room and saw her lying on the bed like a classical French painter's odalisque, I stood still and absorbed my view. I never tired of observing Pearl. She had the sort of beauty that was difficult to put into words. Some women can look hard, chiseled, with a look of ambition cut into their jawbone. Pearl's face struck me as always being so gentle, even though defined. Her nose neat and straight, her cheekbones sweeping up into her perfectly shaped head which was crowned with a thick mane of blonde hair, cut in wavy layers. But it was her eyes that had me mesmerized. Clear and blue, yet the blue would change from a deep ultramarine that almost looked black sometimes, to an almost translucent sky color. Her eyes spoke of innocence and vulnerability: the eyes of a child.

"It's not too late to change your mind, you know. About coming to London with me," I cajoled. She was half asleep. I sat on the edge of the bed and whispered a kiss on her shoulder.

Pearl's eyelids fluttered and I stroked the length of her smooth back, tracing the curve down into her dip and up again over her peachy round buttocks. I could have stared at that ass all day long.

She groaned languidly and parted her legs a touch. Her eyes

flicked open and she smiled lazily. Just touching her soft, silky skin and looking at her beautiful face got me hard again. I wanted to fuck her endlessly. Over and over. I leaned down to kiss her, my tongue parting her full lips, and she responded as her tongue met mine. Slowly, teasingly. I groaned into her mouth—an erotic sound of carnal need vibrated through me. I held her jaw with my hands and deepened the kiss, hungry for more, waiting for her to plead for me to ravage her again. Damn that plane, I was feeling uncontrollably horny. Insatiable. I couldn't get enough of her and felt edgy at the thought of leaving her for just a couple of days. We needed the physical closeness, the frenzied power of orgasms that always hit us simultaneously, that united us.

My eyes scanned down to her hand, flopped by her side, and I took it, feeling her engagement ring between my fingers, mollified that if other men looked at her, at least they'd know she belonged to someone else. *To me.*

"You'd better go or you'll miss your plane," she told me, and I flinched.

"Why are you tormenting me like this? You know I don't like us being apart?"

"I can't just leave Anthony alone," she murmured sleepily.

"Why not? He wouldn't care; he'd have the run of the place, get the staff darting around for him—he'd love it. I don't know why you're going so out of your way for him. He treats you like..." I trailed off—no need, I decided, to point out her brother's failings.

"He's been making more effort lately. That's why he's coming to visit. Anyway, there's another reason I can't go to London: I've got that important meeting with Samuel Myers, you know."

"Sam Myers…the big, fat, Hollywood fish who smokes too many Cuban cigars and calls everyone honey."

Pearl's lips curved into a smile. "I know, he's like a walking cliché from some bad B movie. I want to pitch my buddy movie to him. But I don't want male leads. I want to see a *woman* playing at least one of those parts, maybe both, if I can swing it. I'm so fed up of seeing actresses playing just the love interest."

I squeezed her hand. "Well let's hope he goes for it. I'm proud of you, Pearl, I really am. You're doing a great job of getting HookedUp Enterprises on its feet."

My eyes shifted back to the curves of my fiancée's divine body. I wanted to suggest that another great project would be for her to do a workout video for women over the age of thirty-five; show them that females didn't have to be in their twenties to be in great shape. With Pearl, herself, as the exercise guru—she was a good model for beauty and health. But I never mentioned age to Pearl because I knew that was a soft spot for her. I didn't want to draw attention to the fifteen-year age gap between us, mainly because I never even thought about it myself. Except on occasions like this, when she blew me away with how young she looked, and it annoyed me that people pigeonholed anybody by a number.

She took my hand and kissed it. Soon, I thought, I'd be wearing a wedding ring there. "You'll be late," she warned me again.

"Such a cool customer, aren't you? Sending me off like this

when all I want to do is get right back into bed with you." I ran the top of my finger around the dimples in the small of her back again, tracing it over the mound of her behind and into the luscious, moist valley of her wet folds—a place where I'd spent so many wonderful hours of ecstasy and where I intended to visit for the rest of my life.

"What I like, though," I murmured, my cock rock-hard again, "is when the ice-princess part of you melts." And I whispered in her ear, my fingers deep inside her, "when I fuck the cool-customer nonsense out of you and you lose all self-control. When you whimper and beg me, and scream my name when you come." I eased my fingers out of her again. Let her feel what she'd be missing—have her longing for my return. "Have fun in your meeting, chérie. I'll be keeping tabs on you—just in case you get tempted by sexy Sam."

She laughed and pushed me off the bed. I walked over to my closet and got dressed, slinging on a T-shirt and jeans—I was really late—and when I turned around, Rex had somehow managed to sneak his way onto the bed. Pearl and I had nicknamed him her 'French lover.' I knew he'd be trying to usurp my place when I was gone.

I said goodbye to the pair of them and felt a rush of inexplicable adrenaline coil through my stomach. Leaving my little family behind made me feel nauseous, partly because when I got to London I knew who was waiting for me: Laura.

Like tenacious ivy entwined about an oak tree, Laura just couldn't let me go.

17

I couldn't stop thinking about Pearl. Her image, plus the jet's rumbling and vibrations on the runway before takeoff, were making me fucking horny. I locked the door of my cabin, my cock aching for an orgasm—Pearl fresh in my mind like a haunting painting or photograph that has impacted your soul. It reminded me of my teenage years when I had sex on the brain constantly. That's what Pearl was doing to me.

I undid my jeans and my cock sprang up. *Wait,* I thought, getting my iPhone out of my pocket. *I'll share this with her—make sure she thinks about me while I'm gone. She and I are in this together.*

I remembered entering her from behind, just that morning, fisting her hair to hold her where I wanted her, her soaked core welcoming me as I crammed her full with my thick, heated length, unable to control myself, fucking her probably too hard for her tight, hot kernel. But she still crumbled beneath me, her pussy clenching in a shuddering climax as she dug her nails into the mattress, pushing her butt closer against me….always closer. Both of us craved that intense proximity.

I lay back on the bed in my cabin and put my phone on record mode, holding it close to my huge erection. Then I panned up to my face so she could see my lustful expression. This wasn't going to be live; I'd send it to her when I landed—a little porn movie for her own pleasure. *A keepsake, for when we're old, doddery and gray and I won't be able to get it up any more.*

"I'm thinking of you, chérie," I began, my hand clamped around my stiff cock, "—I should have abducted you and brought you with me." I licked my lips, thinking of her mouth sucking me, flicking her teasing tongue over the broad head of my crest, making me come. "I've got your hot, wet, pearlette in my mind's eye, Pearl, and the expression on your beautiful face when you come for me. Your hard, peaked nipples when I suck them, when I lick you, when I stretch you open and fuck you really hard."

I was moving my hand up and down, tight on my massive erection, jerking it hastily and remembering how, just the day before, I'd come in her mouth, fucking it slowly, and how incredible it felt.

"When I get home, baby, I'm going to tease you with my cock, bend you over and flutter my tongue against your clit. Just the tip of my tongue. You'll be begging me for more and I'll make you wait till you're moaning with anticipation."

What I was doing in that moment felt good but nothing compared to the real thing. I imagined Pearl when she received this little film, would be sitting in her office chair, legs wide open, her fingers inside herself, her other hand massaging her clit, and how I wish I could be there to enter her slowly, the head of my thick cock pushing into her just an inch, then withdrawing and teasing her sensitized cleft, then ramming my whole length into her wet warmth, fucking her hard, then tantalizing her clit again. Over and over, I'd do this, until she was begging for me to fuck her, screaming for me, crying out for her release.

My cock twitched, its broad crown wet with lust. "I'm going to fuck your clit, Pearl, with the tip of my cock, rim it around and around and then cram you full, baby. I'll slip my way in, just an inch, no more. Then thrust it all the way, hard, and then pull almost out. Then tease you again, just a centimeter inside. You won't know when I'm going to slam you. Maybe I'll pump you good and hard, maybe I won't. You'll be screaming for me to fuck you."

My pulse quickened and my breath came heavily—I could feel my impending orgasm about to explode. My fingers squeezed like a vice around the wide crest of my cock and then all the way down to its thick root. "All I can think about is fucking you. I. Love. Fucking. You. Pearl. I love fucking you hard, fucking, you, really slow."

Semen spurted out in a hot rush as the image of Pearl's tits and ass brought harmonies, musical notes of bliss swirling about my brain in an abstract pattern. Like the crescendo of a beautiful aria. Her tits, ass, pussy, nipples, mouth, all one giant billboard in my head. A knock on my cabin door jerked my climax into a tsunami of a wave, coursing through me, and flooding over in abandon.

"I'm coming," I shouted out. *And how.*

The flight attendant said, "Sir, I need you to buckle-up for takeoff."

I was taking off, all right. Really taking off. "Coming," I said again and grinned at the irony of my words.

When I exited my cabin, I nearly had a heart attack. The person sitting right there in my line of vision, neatly and serenely in her seat, was none other than Indira bloody Kapoor, herself. She looked up from her book and said calmly, "Alexandre, how wonderful to see you."

I gazed at her, speechless. *What the fuck was she doing on this plane?* She was wearing a sky-blue sari, draped elegantly about one shoulder and her hair was braided. I had to admit, she looked great. No wonder she was such a big movie star.

"Indira. What a surprise." I walked over, bent down to kiss her on the cheek. "What brings you here on this very *private* plane?"

"I'm like you, Alexandre; I like to hitch-hike on G-5s. So much global warming—always good to spread the wealth a bit, you know, not be too greedy. You were flying to London so I thought I'd hop aboard."

"How did you know I'd be here?" I asked, not even wanting to know what strings she'd pulled.

"A little birdy told me so," she said enigmatically. "You're looking good, Alexandre Chevalier. Truly, you must be one of the most handsome men I think I've ever had the pleasure of working with, including my co-stars. Your eyes—what is it about them? They almost rival mine."

I chuckled. Indira was always good for a laugh. *To work with?* "Well, if you consider the charity work, I guess—"

"Not the charity. You signed that oh, so lucrative piece of

paper giving me power of attorney in India with all things HookedUp," she said coolly, smoothing her braid. I stared at her. She was very composed, very *butter-wouldn't-melt-in-my-mouth.* Her eyes were wide with innocence. Where was this leading?

I sat down next to her, my blood rising, my mind shuffling through possible scenarios with utmost confusion. "No, Indira, I never signed anything of the sort. What are you on about?"

"Oh, but you did. HookedUp is already making waves there and I'm the director."

The flight attendant came by with some hors d'oeuvres and champagne, breaking up our conversation. *What the fuck was Indira playing at?*

"Indira, the only thing you have power of attorney of concerning me, is our charity. A charity which is a *non-profit* organization. A charity which, I hope to God, you will not exploit for your own coffers."

She leaned towards me and, putting her hand on my knee, uncomfortably close to my crotch, whispered, "It's so easy to forge a signature. All you have to do is press the original document against a window with your own on top, and trace over it. Easy peasy pudding and pie. I swear, nobody can tell the two apart. It's even been signed by a notaire, 'witnessed' by two lawyers. I have contacts in high places, as you can imagine. And it's too late now for you to turn the clock back. Of course, if you and I were *real* partners in the true sense of the word, you'd be in on it fifty/fifty."

I laughed. "You're just pulling my leg. Trying to get a reaction out of me." *The woman was nuts. Why did I attract crazy women into my life?*

She arched a dark eyebrow and smirked.

"Indira, Sophie and I sold our India rights of HookedUp to your cousin. I'm out. You, yourself, invested your own money into the HookedUp franchise in India. You wouldn't cut your nose off to spite your own pretty face. You wouldn't jeopardize it. I don't know why you're playing this silly game. I *got* my payment," and I lowered my voice, "I got the gems. That was my deal. Even if you did forge my signature, which I doubt very much, it isn't going to help you."

"Oh, but it will. You watch. My fat little cousin doesn't have full proof of purchase. I do. The company is mine."

"Indira, you're playing with fire. He's not a man to cross." *She wouldn't be so crazy….would she?* My head told me she was spurting a load of nonsense just to rile me, but then I sat up. That cousin could really cause trouble. *Fuck, maybe I do need my bodyguard, after all!* "Really, Indira, if you did what you say you did, you will have gotten yourself into a big, tangled web of a mess."

She adjusted the folds of her sari. "My cousin loves me. In fact, he's *in* love with me. Always has been. I'm family. He'll believe me when I say I was unaware of your gem deal. Because it's true. I wasn't there. I can play dumb. He'll think you double-crossed him."

I closed my eyes in disbelief. *She must be lying.* Whatever, I had no idea what the repercussions would be, but somehow I knew I could end up embroiled in one, big, spicy, tandoori, Bollywood-style banquet of disaster.

Laura. Indira. Who knew? Maybe Claudine would be waiting for my plane to land in London.

I thanked the Lord that Pearl, at least, was normal.

But then a niggling doubt crept into my mind. I'd never had a relationship in my entire life with any woman who was 'normal'—not even my mother was normal. Especially not my mother. And certainly not Sophie.

Why, I asked myself, would Pearl be any different?

Luckily, Indira had a screen test to go to at Shepperton Studios, so we parted ways as soon as we landed. As crazy as my sister drove me, I was glad that she'd be able (I hoped) to come up with some sort of solution for Indira and deal with the cousin. Indira's story was implausible, ridiculous…

But a woman spurned is capable of revenge….history books told us so.

I had a vision of that greasy cousin of hers sending out a sniper to shoot me down, planted on a rooftop somewhere as I went out for an innocent stroll in the park. That part I believed…that he was in love with her. Those large families with cousins and aunts and great uncles and weddings that went on for a whole week, often had incestuous blood snaking through their veins.

I'd have to be alert and on the ball.

18

The purpose of my London visit was to meet an up-and-coming, twenty-three-year-old video game designer, and talk business. I was getting into the video games market, where budgets were bigger than blockbuster feature films and big money could be made. I was a secret player, had been since I was a young boy, although I kept that side of things under wraps. Now, at least, I could use my vice as an excuse. 'Research,' I could say. Boys will be boys. Or rather, men will be boys. When it comes to toys, no man's a grown-up, no matter how hard he pretends.

I also had a meeting with the Minister of Finance from the British government, some of his aides and Sophie. We needed more leeway in Britain. As much as I had threatened Sophie with getting out of HookedUp, I decided to hold off—give her another chance. She'd been making amends with Pearl and her effort seemed genuine. The wedding gown gift proved it. And she'd promised not to let shits like that Russian arms dealer anywhere near our business, so for the moment, I was cool with things.

But I also had other stuff to attend to in England. Of a more personal nature.

Over the last few weeks, I'd listened to several frantic messages from Laura on my voicemail. At first, I ignored them, but as time went on, I decided that I had to deal with the situation. She was threatening to come to New York and I needed to nip that possibility in the bud. She was desperate to see me face-to-face, said she needed to discuss something that couldn't be resolved by phone. She'd been on holiday to my house in Provence, expecting the whole time for me to show up. When I didn't, she really started hounding me.

Poor Laura was obviously hurting. Rationally, my brain told me that it wasn't my problem. Laura was the one who split up with me, dumped me for James—left me to nurse my broken heart. It had been years ago so I was completely over it, but she had no right to play the underdog now. Yet the sympathetic side of me was whispering a different story in my ear: reminding me that she was disabled, only just recently out of a wheelchair. She'd suffered immeasurably and she needed a friend. Since I'd met Pearl, I'd been distant; Laura rarely crossed my mind, but inexplicably I still felt a sense of guilt. So I agreed to meet up. She was going to come and see me at The Connaught where I was staying.

As I was mulling all this over, taking a shortcut through St. James's Park on my way back to the hotel, like a bolt of lightening, I remembered my niece. I'd been so wrapped up in Pearl, and Sophie's dodgy business antics over the past couple of months that I'd forgotten to check up on Elodie. I'd seen her around the office building in Manhattan but we hadn't had a chance to talk. She'd asked for security so I'd provided my bodyguard to be on call for her whenever she wanted him. I'd never actually used him for myself but had him on my payroll just for good measure. Maybe, I'd be asking for his help now, though, after Indira's shenanigans.

I called and waited for Elodie to pick up. My walk was a welcome relief, away from the city's traffic and noise. As I looked around, I noted that there was a difference between the parks in London and Paris, a clue to the discrepancy in nature between both countries. Paris was so formal; people were forbidden to loll about the grass in the parks of central Paris—but in London you saw kids play football, dogs chasing ducks and geese, and people sprawled out sunbathing, or enjoying a picnic.

It was lunch hour and office workers were eating sandwiches and basking in the crisp autumnal sunshine, away from the confines of their stuffy offices, the tyranny of their computers and petty internal politics—the perils of a nine-to-five job. As I was listening to Elodie's ring tone, I people-watched and dog-watched. Why wasn't she picking up?

She finally answered. "Elodie," I said, relieved that she hadn't changed her number. "What took you so long? And why haven't you called to check in?"

"I'm sorry," she replied in a bored drawl, "just put the roses over there, would you? I've been busy with stuff."

"Roses?"

"Just a delivery," and she added quickly, "for my roommate."

"Is everything okay?"

"Yeah, it's okay now. Things are better."

"You're not still scared? Not worried about being followed?"

"No, no," and then she said with a faint giggle, "I was imagining things. Everything's fine."

My eye caught the view of the London Eye in the distance, peeking out above the golden and russet-colored trees. "You're sure?" I checked again. There was something in her tone that I found disarming. A beat of silence at her end of the line was muffled by cries of geese near the park's small lake. I thought about the position of where I stood in that moment; Buckingham Palace at one side, and at the other, the Foreign Office and 10 Downing Street where the British Prime Minister lived. I imagined several M15 spies had their meetings right here, away from bugs and walls with ears—spyware everywhere. They, too, were spying on others for a living. And I wondered, once again, if I should do my own share of espionage; have Elodie followed for her own safety, or if that was breaching her privacy too much.

Because something made me suspect that when she said that everything was okay, she was lying.

I relaxed back into the sofa of my penthouse at The Connaught, described by the hotel as, 'London's most luxurious home.' I was enjoying a power nap. I have always been a fan of the nanosecond siesta—it can do wonders. There was a knock at the door. Odd, the concierge always called first and room service had already passed by that morning. I hadn't ordered anything, hadn't summoned the butler. I looked at my watch. Laura wasn't due for another forty minutes. I had specifically arranged for us to meet downstairs—I didn't want the intimacy of her being in my living quarters. I knew Laura, her persuasiveness, her doggedness. When she wanted something, she usually got it, and right now, I sensed she wanted me.

My heart started racing. *Fuck—Indira's cousins—the London lot—Indians always have relatives in London. Perhaps a clan of them are waiting outside my door with crowbars, ready to top me off.*

I called reception. "Hello, Mr. Chevalier here. Did anyone ask to come up and see me?"

"No, sir," the concierge replied.

Just at that moment, there was another knock at the door and a voice, which I knew well, cried out, "Alexandre, it's me. I know you're in there, let me in."

Bloody hell. It was Laura.

Being so relieved that it wasn't a bunch of furious uncles about to launch an attack, I let Laura in. She looked taller than usual, or perhaps I had just gotten used to Pearl. Laura seemed Amazonian in comparison—she was at least six foot two in heels. Her blonde hair flowed down her back and her bee-stung lips pouted at me like a small child who was determined to get her daddy's attention.

"Alex, why the look of suspicion on your face? You look like you've seen a ghost." She stepped into the room and threw her white cashmere coat onto an armchair. She looked like a supermodel: tall, skinny. Swaggering with confidence, even though she was using a cane and had a very slight limp. The cane was black with a mother-of-pearl handle, so it matched her glamorous outfit.

"How did you get past reception?"

"Oh please," she murmured, as if I'd said the dumbest thing in the world. She thrust her shoulders back and stuck out her chest. She wasn't wearing a bra and her nipples pointed sharp under her flimsy silk blouse. "Well, aren't you going to kiss me hello?"

I came over to her and offered a peck on the cheek. She responded with a soft, damp kiss. "I've missed you darling," she breathed into my ear.

"Shame Pearl couldn't be here," I said in reply, walking to the other end of the room and sitting on a couch. "She would have loved to have met you." *Not.*

"So how's your mum?" she said, totally ignoring my comment.

"Fine. I saw her in Paris a couple of months ago. Or was it just last month? Time flies."

"Yes, time does fly. Especially when you're suffering." She looked down at the floor.

"I'm sorry if things haven't turned out the way you wanted, Laura. But you're looking great. I see you're on your feet again. You should be proud of yourself. So, what was it that was so important and couldn't wait? What did you want to talk to me about?"

She flicked her long hair. "I've always been curious to see this famous penthouse apartment at The Connaught." She surveyed her surroundings with approval. "Nice. Very chic. I'll go and check out the balcony in a moment, when I've caught my breath. I have to say, it's stunning. I could quite happily move in."

"Your house is hardly a hovel," I said, realizing she was in the mood to play the beat-around-the-bush game.

"Aren't you going to offer me a drink?"

"Yes, of course. A soft drink?"

"God, no. I need a *real* drink."

"Should I call the butler? Or better still, we can go downstairs."

"No. God, no. Let's just keep it us, shall we, and stay right here."

I stood up and made my way to the bar. I turned around. "What would you like, then?"

She shuffled on the edge of the armchair and I saw a flash of her panties. Bare legs, apart from killer-heeled, thigh high, black leather boots. Probably Gucci. She loved Gucci. A mini skirt. She had modeled pantyhose once—her legs didn't seem to end.

"Something expensive," she said.

"What?"

"I don't know, you choose. A bottle of chilled Cristal? A vintage Bordeaux? Nothing too plebian. Something I don't drink at home."

"Laura, you and James have the best-stocked drinks' cabinet in London!"

"Surprise me. *Impress* me."

I had forgotten that about Laura. She was high-maintenance. I'd been constantly scrambling about to please her when we dated. Wanted to make her proud of me. Tried to treat her like the queen she felt she was. But that was when I was twenty. I had grown up a bit since then.

"I have no idea what will impress you, Laura."

"What about a Bloody Mary, how about that?"

"Okay," I agreed. "Good idea." It did seem a fitting drink for her, but in that moment I didn't know why. "Living in New York has trained my taste buds," I said. "They know how to make a kickass Bloody Mary there. Lots of horseradish sauce and the right amount of spice."

"Kickass? Ugh, you're picking up some really tacky American expressions, Alex." And then she mumbled, "Must be that….that…" She didn't finish her sentence, just sneered, and then continued, "Actually, let *me* make the Bloody Marys. I bet I can outdo those New York bartenders."

"I bet you can't, but be my guest, give it a go—I need to make some calls."

I went out onto the balcony and took in the views over Mayfair, wondering how I could get this too-cozy-for-comfort rendezvous over with as quickly as possible. I didn't often drink midday but what the hell, I thought. Maybe Laura had started self-medicating with booze because of the physical pain she was in, so no harm in joining her—my important meetings for the day were safely out of the way.

I called various work contacts. Then, as I was chatting to someone in Rome about a share in a boutique hotel I had there, Laura came out and handed me my Bloody Mary.

"Here we go," she whispered. "Don't want to interrupt your call. Don't mind me, I'll entertain myself with a magazine or something, while you take care of business."

I watched her out of the corner of my eye as she moved off toward the dining room, aided by her cane. The place was vast: a dining room with seating for ten, two bedrooms, two bathrooms and a large living room. Fresh flowers in bespoke vases, oil paintings adorning the walls, strategically placed at eye level. Creams and pale blues and, oh, so very Laura—I knew she'd be impressed and would want to nose about. That's why she'd insisted on coming up and not meeting me in the lobby, I thought. I sipped my Bloody Mary. Actually, it was very good; she'd gotten the recipe right, after all.

I called Sophie.

"Did you deal with Indira?" I asked her when she picked up.

"She's full of shit—she was just winding you up, Alexandre. Of course she hasn't forged your signature."

"I thought as much. Did she admit that?"

"In so many words. I'm having tea with her today at The Ritz, just to smooth things over. Want to join us? We could pass by and pick you up."

"No, don't. Please, *you* deal with her, Sophie. I don't want hoards of angry relatives hunting me down. Right now, I have other issues which I need to sort out. I'll be back in New York tomorrow. I'll call you then."

I could have sworn I heard water running. I made my way to where the sound was coming from, and lo and behold, Laura was running a bath. Worse, she was *in* the bath. Nude. There, in the pristine, all-white bathroom was an oval tub, smack bang in the middle of the room. Laura was lying right in it, coated in frothy bubbles, splashing about.

"Jesus, Laura, what the fuck are you doing?"

"Ssh, Alex, don't shout. I thought I'd have a little soak, that's all. Don't get your knickers in a twist."

I don't wear knickers. I turned around, my back to her; *this* view of London, Laura nude, had not been on my agenda. "Laura, you're not even meant to be up here; we were meant to meet *downstairs*. Fine, pop by to say hello, but you can't just fucking *move* in on me!"

"Alex, I'm in pain! Why do I have to keep reminding you of this? Have you any idea what it's like…your muscles aching and pinching and throbbing all the time? I just need a hot soak to make me feel better. Will you be an angel and fetch me my Bloody Mary? I left it in the living room by mistake."

"Laura, *please*."

"Bring me my drink, Alex, and stop being such a bore. Oh yes, and a magazine. I forgot that, too. *Vogue* or *Interiors*. Nothing tacky."

"Laura, please. I'm engaged to be married! *You're* married. Fine, we can still be friends, but you *in the bath at my hotel?* This is going beyond the boundaries of friendship—this is *too fucking much!*"

"Alex darling, please stop being such a pleb. Just bring me my drink and magazine, I'll have a nice quiet soak and then I'll leave. Or better still: *join* me. This bath is big enough for two."

She was incorrigible but I knew that the only way to get her out of that bathtub would be to physically manhandle her, which I wasn't about to do. "Ten minutes," I warned. "Then it's time for you to leave. You said you had something important to discuss but that was obviously a ruse to hang out with me. I can't just *hang out* anymore, Laura. Not like this. Pearl and I are getting *married*."

"Yeah right. Winter's a long way away."

I turned around in surprise. She was sitting up, erect, with her chest out, her breasts little and pert—she was fluttering her eyelashes at me, and smiling.

"How do you know that?" I demanded, turning my back on her again. I don't know why I even bothered—I'd seen it all before.

"Oh you know, Elodie and I chat every so often. I call her for news once in a while."

In-fucking-corrigible. I drained my Bloody Mary—the kick of alcohol felt good—I needed it to ease my irritation. "Ten minutes, Laura. I'm not bringing you your drink and any magazines because making things more comfortable for you here is *not* my intention."

"Alex, you *will* come around, darling, believe me. Because I have a little surprise for you."

I narrowed my eyes with suspicion. "Like what?"

"Ooh, that would be telling."

"I've got work to do. I'm going next door. Ten. Minutes. Only. Then I'm sending you home in a cab."

I left the bathroom, wondering how I'd forgotten about Laura's manipulative ways. Still, it was nothing I couldn't handle….

Or so I thought.

The next thing I knew, I'd fallen asleep on the sofa. I tried to shift myself but felt all floppy. I realized my arms were above my head, tied together with some sort of wire cable. In fact, *all* of me felt buzzy and floppy, except the one part of my anatomy which mattered most. When I finally focused, I saw Laura on top of me, pinning me down like a vice—her nude body straddling me, her long knees digging into the sofa either side of my hips. A scar ran down her left thigh where they'd operated on her after her accident. My eyes flicked down. The buttons of my jeans were open, my shirt, open. Fuck! My dick was mysteriously rock-hard and she was about to ease herself on top of me.

Laura, what the fuck are you doing? I thought I said the words, but all that came from my lips was a sort of incoherent groan.

She pushed back my head as I attempted to get up. "Ssh, Alex, just relax. All you have to do is lie there, darling, I'll do the work."

Madonna's *Frozen* was playing, ringing in my ears. How apt, considering every cell in my body felt numb. Laura's long blonde hair was flopping over me, her lips centimeters away from mine.

"Hmm, I'd forgotten how good you smell," she purred.

She had my cock firmly in one hand and was guiding it towards her pussy like a rocket aimed for liftoff.

Any second now, that rocket was about to be launched.

Pearl Playlist

Can't Get Enough Of Your Love Baby – Barry White

Let's Stay Together – Al Green

Sex Bomb – Tom Jones

Can't Help Falling In Love – Elvis Presley

Sex Machine – James Brown

Feeling Good – Nina Simone

Can't Take My Eyes off You – Frankie Valli and The 4 Seasons

Wonderful Tonight – Eric Clapton

Mission Impossible Theme

Personal Jesus – Johnny Cash

Miss You – The Rolling Stones

Je T'aime…Moi Non Plus – Jane Birkin & Serge Gainsbourg

Manhattan Serenade – Jo Stafford

Frozen – Madonna

Part 2 of ***Pearl*** will be released October 2013.

Want to be the first to know what happens next? Sign up (http://ariannerichmonde.com/email-signup/) to be informed the minute the next book, or any future Arianne Richmonde releases, go live. Your details are private and will not be shared with anyone. You can unsubscribe at any time.

I have also written Glass, a short story.

Join me on Facebook:
https://www.facebook.com/AuthorArianneRichmonde

Join me on Twitter:
https://twitter.com/a_richmonde

For more information about me, visit my website:
http://ariannerichmonde.com/

If you would like to email me:
mailto:ariannerichmonde@gmail.com